The Beggar

The following titles by Naguib Mahfouz
are also published by Doubleday
and Anchor Books:

THE THIEF AND THE DOGS

THE BEGINNING AND THE END

WEDDING SONG

PALACE WALK

AUTUMN QUAIL

RESPECTED SIR

NAGUIB MAHFOUZ

The Beggar

Translated by
Kristin Walker Henry
and
Nariman Khales Naili al-Warraki

Doubleday

New York   London   Toronto   Sydney   Auckland

PUBLISHED BY DOUBLEDAY
a division of Bantam Doubleday Dell Publishing Group, Inc.
666 Fifth Avenue, New York, New York 10103

DOUBLEDAY and the portrayal of an anchor with a dolphin
are trademarks of Doubleday, a division of Bantam Doubleday Dell
Publishing Group, Inc.

This English translation was first published by The American University
in Cairo Press in 1986. First published in Arabic as *al-Shahhādh* in 1965.
Protected under the Berne Convention. The Doubleday edition is
published by arrangement with The American University in Cairo Press.

Library of Congress Cataloging-in-Publication Data
Maḥfūẓ, Najīb, 1911–
   [Shaḥḥādh. English]
   The beggar / Naguib Mahfouz; translated by
   Kristin Walker Henry
   and Nariman Khales Naili al-Warraki.
   —1st Doubleday ed.
      p. cm.
   Translation of: al-Shahhādh.
   I. Title.
PJ7846.A46S413 1990   89-48672
892'.736—dc20   CIP
ISBN 0-385-26455-0
ISBN 0-385-26456-9 (pbk.)

FOREWORD

"The trouble with most modern Arabic literature," I have frequently heard Western editors complain, "is that it's always about politics." The complaint itself is interesting, not only in what it presumes to be important but also in the historical attitude it implies toward even Western literature, in which from the ancient Greeks onward politics has been a central subject during every period—except perhaps the Dark Ages. What would the Dante of the *Inferno* or the Shakespeare of the Histories make of this complaint, for example, not to mention Milton, whose Council in Pandemonium remains our finest description of a Cabinet debate? What, for that matter, would a V. S. Naipaul or a Gabriel García Márquez have to say? One suspects that in this instance, as in so many others, special rules of some sort have been devised for application to Arabs only.

The Beggar is an ironic case in point, since few Western readers coming to it or to Mahfouz for the first time are likely to understand that it, too, like "most modern Arabic literature," is a political book. First published in 1965, when Mahfouz was in his mid-fifties, it belongs to a remarkable series of novels (*The Children of Gebelawi, The Thief and the Dogs, Autumn Quail, The Path, Small Talk on the Nile,* and *Miramar*) in which he tried to assess the impact of political change upon the country he had known before the Revolution of July 1952.

Though his famous Cairo Trilogy was published between 1954 and 1957, Mahfouz had in fact composed its last words in 1952, then stopped writing for more than five years. "The world I had made it my mission to describe," he told Philip

Stewart, one of his translators, "had disappeared." When a new work—*The Children of Gebelawi*—finally appeared in 1959, it created a scandal, not only because of its subject matter but also because of its technique, which represented a complete abandonment of the old-fashioned descriptive novel. Making allegorical use of religious history, it suggested that the new regime would ultimately not be much different from the old ones; and did so with a passionate, darting intelligence that seemed to have turned political disappointment—even despair—into a new freedom of expression.

Despair is the keynote of the series of six novels that followed, which ended with the debacle of the Six-Day War in 1967. Omar, the protagonist of *The Beggar*, belongs to the class and the generation that should have provided Egypt with leadership, but have instead been deprived of any significant function. His old classmates Mustapha and Othman, who are in some sense his alter egos, suggest the dangers of either accommodation or opposition, while Omar himself suggests one of the causes of their irrelevance: failure to care enough at the right time. Their liberal secularism, the central motif in Egyptian higher culture for the previous hundred years, of which they represent a kind of culmination, has simply been shelved as an operative ideal, though it may survive as an irrepressible yearning. It thus finds indirect expression, necessarily inadequate, as sex or poetry, though even in a Voltairean garden one can never be saved by such longings.

The Beggar then is a complex and passionate outcry against irrelevance and against what is likely to follow—alienation. Surely it is about things that matter; and matter in places other than the Arab world.

JOHN RODENBECK

The Beggar

ONE

White clouds floated in the blue expanse overlooking a vast green land where cows grazed serenely. Nothing indicated what country it was. In the foreground a child, mounted on a wooden horse, gazed toward the horizon, a mysterious semi-smile in his eyes. Omar wondered idly who did the painting as he sat alone in the waiting room. It was almost time for the appointment he'd made ten days earlier. The table in the middle of the room was strewn with newspapers and magazines; dangling over the edge was the photo of a woman accused of kidnapping children. He turned back to amuse himself with the painting—a pasture, cows, a child, the horizon. Although the painting had little value apart from its ornamental gold frame, he liked the searching child, the tranquil cows. But Omar's condition was worsening, his eyelids were heavy and his heartbeats sluggish. There the child looks at the horizon, and how tightly it grips the earth, closes in upon the earth from any angle you observe it. What an infinite prison. Why the wooden horse, why the cows so full of tranquillity? Steady footsteps sounded in the hall outside, and then the male nurse appeared at the door, saying, "Come in, please."

Would his old school friend recognize him after a quarter of a century? He entered the office of the distinguished physician. There he stood, smiling, a dark slender man with kinky hair and glowing eyes. He had hardly changed from their days in the school courtyard. The corner of his mouth had the same ironic turn, suggesting his old gaiety and sharp wit.

"Welcome, Omar. You've changed, but for the better!"

"I didn't think you'd remember me."

They shook hands warmly.

"What a giant you are! You were always very tall but now that you've put on weight you've become enormous," he said, raising his head to Omar.

Omar smiled with pleasure and repeated, "I really didn't think you'd remember me."

"But I don't forget anyone, so how could I forget you?"

It was a gracious welcome from one in his position. After all, a distinguished physician is widely renowned; who hears of the lawyer other than those with legal cases?

The physician laughed while surveying him and said, "You really have put on weight. You look like a business tycoon from the past, nothing missing except the cigar!"

A grin appeared on Omar's dark, full face. Slightly abashed, he settled his glasses in place while raising his thick eyebrows.

"I'm happy to meet you again, Doctor."

"And I you, though the occasion of seeing me is not usually pleasant."

He returned to his desk, which was piled with books, papers, and various instruments and gestured to Omar to take a seat.

"Let's leave our reminiscences until after we've reassured ourselves about your health." He opened his case book and started to write. "Name: Omar al-Hamzawi. Profession: Lawyer. Age?" The physician laughed, saying in anticipation, "Don't worry, we're in the same predicament."

"Forty-five."

"Remember what a difference in age a month seemed when we were in school? But now, who cares? Any history of special illness in the family?"

"None, unless you consider high blood pressure after sixty extraordinary."

The physician folded his arms and said seriously, "Let's hear what you've got."

Omar stroked his thick black hair, in which the first strands of white were discernible, and said, "I don't believe I'm ill in the usual sense."

The physician regarded him attentively.

"I mean I don't have the usual symptoms . . ."

"Yes."

"But I feel a strange lethargy."

"Is that all?"

"I think so."

"Perhaps it's overwork."

"I'm not sure that's the answer."

"Of course not. Otherwise you wouldn't have honored me with your visit."

"In fact, I no longer feel any desire to work at all."

"Go on."

"It's not fatigue. I suppose I could still work, but I have no desire to, no desire at all. I've left the work to the assistant lawyer in my office and postponed all my own cases for the past month . . ."

"Haven't you thought of taking a vacation?"

Omar continued as though he hadn't heard. "Very often I'm sick of life, people, even the family. The situation seemed too serious to keep silent."

"Then the problem is not . . ."

"The problem is very serious. I don't want to think, to move, or to feel. Everything is disintegrating and dying. My hope in coming here was to find some physical cause."

The physician remarked with a smile, "If only we could solve our most serious problems with a pill after eating or a spoonful of medicine before sleeping."

They proceeded into the examination room. Omar took off his clothes and lay down on the medical cot. The physician followed the usual procedure. He looked at Omar's out-stretched tongue, then pressed up his eyelids and examined his eyes, took his blood pressure, then measured his breathing with the stethoscope. Omar breathed deeply, coughed, and said "Ah" once from the throat, again from the chest, and glanced furtively at the physician's face without reading anything. The elegant fingers then tapped on his chest and on his back and pressed with more force on his abdomen. The examination over, the physician returned to his office, where Omar joined him a few minutes later. He finished looking at the results of the urine analysis taken earlier, rubbed his hands, smiled broadly, and said, "My dear lawyer, there's absolutely nothing."

The nostrils of his long, sharp nose dilated and his face flushed. "Nothing at all?"

"At all," the physician affirmed, but added cautiously, "I'm afraid the problem may be more serious." Then he laughed. "Though it's not a case which can be exaggerated to double the fees!"

Omar laughed while looking at him expectantly.

"Well, then," the doctor stressed, "you should know that it's nothing but . . ."

Omar asked uneasily, "Is the psychiatric ward my fate, then?"

"Neither a psychiatric nor any other kind of ward."

"Really?"

"Yes. You've got a bourgeois disease, if I may use the term our newspapers are so fond of. You're not sick," he continued more slowly, "but I see the first signs of something more than a disease. You've come at the appropriate time. When did the lethargy appear?"

"Two months ago, perhaps a bit earlier, but for the last month it's been agonizing."

"Let me describe your life as I see it. You're a successful, wealthy man. You've virtually forgotten how to walk. You eat the best food, drink good wine, and have overburdened yourself with work to the point of exhaustion. Your mind is preoccupied with your clients' cases and your own holdings. Anxiety about the future of your work and your financial situation has got the better of you."

Omar gave a slight laugh and said, "That's the picture, in general, but now I've lost interest in everything."

"Well, there's nothing wrong with you for the time being, but the enemy lurks on the border."

"Like Israel?"

"And if we don't take care, serious danger may overwhelm us."

"We're getting to the point."

"Be moderate in your eating, drink less, stick to regular exercise such as walking, and there'll be no grounds for fear."

Omar waited, thinking, but the doctor said no more. "Aren't you going to write me a prescription?"

"No. You're not a villager who needs a superfluous prescription to be convinced of my importance. The real cure is in your hands alone."

"I'll be my old self again?"

"And better ... In spite of my heavy load of work at the university and the hospital and clinic, I walk every day for at least a half hour and I watch my diet."

"I've never felt the advance of years."

"Old age is a disease which you won't feel as long as you follow a sensible regime. There are youths of over sixty. The important thing is to understand life."

"To understand life?"

"I'm not speaking philosophically, of course."

"But your treatment of me is based on some sort of philosophy. Hasn't it ever occurred to you to question the meaning of your life?"

The physician laughed loudly and said, "I have no time for that. As long as I serve those in need each hour, what meaning does the question have?" Then he advised, with friendly concern, "Take a vacation."

"My vacation is usually so interrupted that the summer months hardly seem more than one prolonged weekend."

"No, take a real vacation, practice the new regime, and you'll be on the road to recovery."

"Perhaps."

"Trust in God. You've been given a warning from nature. Listen to it. You should lose forty pounds, but gradually, and without strain."

Omar pressed his hands on his knees and leaned foward in preparation to leave, but the doctor responded quickly, "Wait, you're the last visitor today, so let's sit together a while."

Omar sat back in his seat smiling. "Dr. Hamid Sabri, I know what you want—to bury a quarter of a century and laugh again from the depths of your heart."

"Ah, the days of the past."

"Actually, Doctor, all periods except 'now' have their appeal."

"You're right. Memory is one thing, the experience another."

"So it all passes and scatters without meaning."

"Our love of life gives meaning."

"How I've detested life these last days!"

"And now you're searching for your lost love. Tell me, do you remember those days of politics, demonstrations, and dreams of Utopia?"

"Of course, but those too have passed and are not held in much esteem these days."

"Even so, a great dream was realized. I mean the socialist state."

"Yes . . ."

The doctor smiled. "You're a man of many faces: the fervent socialist, the great lawyer, but the face I remember most vividly is that of Omar the poet."

Omar dissembled his sudden agitation with a wan smile. "That's unfortunate."

"You've abandoned poetry?"

"Of course."

"But, as I remember, you published a collection of poems."

He lowered his eyes so that the doctor wouldn't see his tension and discontent. "Childhood play, nothing more."

"Some of my physician colleagues have given up medicine for the sake of poetry."

The memory disturbed his consciousness like ill-omened weather. He wished the doctor would drop the subject.

"I remember one of our friends was Mustapha al-Minyawi. What was it we called him?"

"Little Baldy. We're still very close friends. He's now a prominent journalist and writes for radio and television."

"My wife is a great fan of his. He was an enthusiastic socialist like you, but the most committed of all, without question, was Othman Khalil."

Omar's face clouded as memory hammered at him. He murmured, "He's in jail."

"Yes, he's spent a long time in jail. Wasn't he your classmate in the Faculty of Law?"

"We graduated in the same year, Mustapha, Othman, and I. I don't really like the past."

The physician said decisively, "So take an interest in the future." Then, looking at his watch: "From now on you're the doctor."

In the waiting room, Omar raised his eyes once again to the picture. The child was still riding his wooden horse, gazing at the horizon. Was it this which prompted his mysterious smile? The horizon still closed in upon the earth. What did the beams of starlight traveling millions of light-years perceive? There are questions which no doctor can answer.

Outside the building he climbed into his black Cadillac, which floated away from the square like a bark on the Nile.

TWO

The faces peered at him expectantly even before they'd exchanged greetings. Their concern was sincere, and he was troubled by his dissatisfaction, the bitterness which spoiled the remaining affection. Behind them the balcony overlooked the Nile. He focused on his wife's thick neck above her white collar and on her fleshy cheeks. She stood as the pillar of faith and virtue. Her green eyes were pouched in fat, but her smile was innocent and affectionate as she said, "My heart tells me all is well."

Mustapha al-Minyawi stood beside her in his sharkskin suit, his slender build overshadowed by her sturdiness. His pale oval face, lackluster eyes, and bald head were turned toward Omar.

"Tell us about our old school friend. What did he say? Did he recognize you?"

Buthayna stood with her elbow leaning on the shoulder of a bronze statue, the statue of a woman stretching out her arms in welcome. Her green eyes looked at her father expectantly. She had the fine figure of her mother when she was fourteen, but it seemed unlikely that she would grow obese with the years, that she would allow fat to mar her beauty. As was often the case, the glance in her eyes expressed an unspoken communication. Jamila, her younger sister, played with her teddy bear between two armchairs, oblivious of his arrival.

They all sat down and he said calmly, "Nothing."

Zeinab exclaimed gratefully, "Thank God. How many times did I say that you only needed rest?"

Her complacency exasperated him. Pointing to his wife, he said to Mustapha, "The responsibility is hers." And he repeated the charge after summarizing the doctor's remarks.

Mustapha said gleefully, "This is no more than play therapy!" But then he added ruefully, "Except for food and drinking. Curse them."

Why should he curse them? He's not the one affected. The one who sets out on the mysterious voyage, perplexed by love and dissatisfaction, unable to speak to himself in a suitable language, what is *he* to do? Omar said to Mustapha, "Dr. Hamid asked about Baldy." After the burst of laughter had subsided, he added, "And congratulations on winning his wife's admiration."

Mustapha grinned boyishly, displaying his white teeth. "Thanks to the radio and TV, I've developed into a plague, striking those with weak resistance."

Omar reflected about his other friend in jail. Ennui dulls even the sensitive conscience. Omar had been in the heat of danger, but his friend had not confessed. In spite of torture, he had not confessed. Now he'd melted into the darkness as though he'd never existed, while Omar grew sick with luxury, and his wife had become the exemplary symbol of the kitchen and the bank. Ask yourself whether the Nile beneath us doesn't despair.

"Papa, should we get ready to travel?"

"We'll have a great time. I'm going to teach your sister to swim as I once taught you."

"Away to the life buoys."

Here is your mother resembling a giant life buoy. How oppressive the horizon is. Freedom is hidden somewhere beyond it and no hope remains except a troubled conscience.

"Unfortunately my wife prefers the beach at Ras el Bar, and someone like me never gets a vacation unless he's stricken with cancer."

Jamila raised her head from her teddy bear, asking, "When will we leave, Papa?"

Mustapha was a monument to his love and marriage; counselor, helper, and witness. Every day he proved anew his friendship to Omar and the family. As yet he knew nothing of the waters which drifted in the river's depths.

"The doctor reminded me of my poetical youth!"

Mustapha laughed. "It seems he hasn't heard of my recent dramatic masterpieces."

"I wish I'd told him of your experiences with art."

"I wonder if the great physician believes in art."

"His wife is fond of you. Isn't that enough?"

"Then she's fond of watermelon seeds and popcorn."

Zeinab, who'd been watching the servant through the arched doorway, then said, "Let's go in to dinner."

Omar announced that he would restrict himself to a chicken breast, fruit, and one glass of whiskey, to which Mustapha replied, "How about the caviar? Do I consume it alone?" Then he proceeded to give the description of Churchill's breakfast which appeared in one of the newspapers during his visit to Cyprus. Although Omar hesitated a bit at the beginning of the meal, he soon ate and drank without restraint. Zeinab likewise couldn't resist temptation and drank a whole bottle of beer. Buthayna ate with moderation, a perversity in the eyes of her mother.

Mustapha remarked, "Food offers a better explanation of human behavior than sex does."

Omar forgot himself for the first time, exclaiming merrily, "It seems you've got chickenitis!"

After dinner they sat together for half an hour, then Jamila was taken to bed and Buthayna and her mother went to visit friends in the same building. So Omar and Mustapha were left alone on the large balcony, a bottle of whiskey and an ice bucket on the glass-topped table between them. Not a movement stirred the trees and the lamps were covered with a veil of sand. The Nile appeared through the gaps of the treetops, silent, pale, devoid of life and meaning. Mustapha drank alone and muttered despairingly, "One hand on its own does not clap."

Omar said, lighting a cigarette, "It's awful weather, and nothing pleases me anymore."

Mustapha laughed. "I remember you couldn't stand me at one time."

Omar disregarded the interruption. "I'm afraid my attitude toward work will continue indefinitely."

"If you stick to your diet and exercise, you won't indulge in despair and let Buthayna down."

"I'm going to drink another glass."

"Okay, but you'll have to be stricter in Alexandria."

"What do you mean, I couldn't stand you? You're a liar like most of those who practice your profession."

"You were disgusted with me at the time of my great commitment to art."

"I was undergoing an agonizing conflict within myself."

"Yes, you were battling a secret urge which you suppressed cruelly, and my commitment must have been alarming to you."

"But I never despised you; I found in you simply a tortured conscience."

"I respected your conflict and forgave you, determined to keep you and art." Then Mustapha laughed and said, "You must have been reassured when I decided to forsake art. Here I am, selling watermelon seeds and popcorn via the mass media, while you scale the summit of the legal profession in Al-Azhar Square."

Repeated memories as stifling as the summer heat and the perennial dust revolve in a closed cycle. The child imagines he's riding a genuine horse. "He was exasperated, he is exasperated, be exasperated, so he is exasperated, she is exasperated, and the plural is they are exasperated."

"Diet and sports."

"You're a riot."

"Amusement is my mission in life, and the plural is amusements. Art had meaning in the past, but science intruded and destroyed its significance."

"I deserted art without being influenced by science."

"Why did you give it up, then?"

He's as aggravating as the summer heat. The night lacked personality and merriment. There was noise in the street. How clever he is, posing questions to which he knows the answer. "Let me ask you the reason."

"You told me at the time you wanted to live well and succeed."

"So why did you ask the question?"

A look of recognition flickered in the eyes dulled by a past illness.

"You yourself didn't give up art for the sake of science alone."

"Enlighten me further."

"You couldn't create art that measured up to science."

Mustapha laughed with an abandon bestowed by the whiskey and said, "Escape is always partly caused by failure, but believe me, science has robbed art of everything. In science you find the rapture of poetry, the ecstasy of religion, and the aspirations of philosophy. All that is left to art is amusement. One day it will be no more than a bridal ornament worn during the honeymoon."

"This marvelous indictment springs from a revenge against art rather than a love of science."

"Read the astronomy, physics, or other science texts, recall whatever plays and collections of poetry you wish, and note the sense of shame which overwhelms you."

"Similar to my feelings when I think of legal cases and the law."

"It's only the feeling of the artist out of step with time."

Omar yawned, then said, "Damn it, I smell something serious in the air, and I have the horrible feeling that a building is going to be demolished."

Mustapha filled a new glass and said, "We won't let the building be demolished."

Omar leaned toward him and asked, "What do you think is wrong with me?"

"Exhaustion, monotony, and time."

"Will diet and sports be enough?"

"More than enough, rest assured."

THREE

From now on you're the doctor and you're free. Freedom of action is a type of creativity, even while you're struggling against the appetites. If we say that man was not created to gorge himself with food, then with the liberation of the stomach the spirit is free to soar. Thus the clouds grow limpid and the August storms thunder. But how oppressive are the crowds, the humidity, and the smell of sweat. The exercise exhausted you and your feet ached as though you were learning how to walk for the first time. Eyes stared as the giant slowed his steps and, overcome by fatigue, sat down on the nearest bench on the Corniche. After a quarter of a century's blindness, you looked at people again. Thus had the shore witnessed the birth of Adam and Eve, but no one knows who will emerge from paradise. As a tall, thin youth, the son of a petty employee, he'd walked the length and breadth of Cairo without complaint, and generations of his ancestors had bruised their feet struggling with the land and had collapsed in the end from fatigue. Soon the past will emerge from prison, and existence will become more of a torment.

"Othman, why are you looking at me like that?"

"Don't you want to play ball?"

"I don't like sports."

"Nothing except poetry?"

Where can one escape your piercing glance? What's the use of arguing with you? You know that poetry is my life and that the coupling of two lines begets a melody which makes the wings of heaven dance.

"Isn't that so, Mustapha?"

The balding adolescent stated, "Existence itself is nothing but a composition of art."

One day Othman in a state of revelation proclaimed, "I found the magic solution to all our problems." Trembling with fervor, we raced up the heights of Utopia. The poetry meters were disrupted by convulsive explosions. We agreed that our souls were worthless. We proposed a gravitational force, other than Newton's, around which the living and dead revolved in an imaginary balance; none rising above or falling beneath the others. But when other forces opposed us, we preferred comfort to failure and thus the giant climbed with extraordinary speed from a Ford to a Packard until he settled in the end in a Cadillac and was on the verge of drowning in a quagmire of fat.

The umbrellas with their tassels touching each other formed a huge multicolored dome under which semi-nude bodies reclined. The pungent smell of perspiration dispersed in the bracing sea air under a sun which had renounced its tyranny. Buthayna stood smiling, a slim wet figure with red arms and legs, her hair shoved under a blue nylon cap. He himself was almost naked, the bushy black hair of his chest exposed to the sun. Jamila was sitting between his legs building a sand pyramid. Zeinab reclined on a leather chaise longue stitching rose petals on an embroidery frame, her healthy bulk and swelling breasts inviting the stares of imbecilic adolescents.

Dear Mustapha,

I read your weekly review of the arts. It was superb—both witty and provocative. You say you're a mere vendor of melon seeds and popcorn, but your inherent discernment and your long experience as a serious critic are evident. Even in jest you write with style. Thanks for your letter inquiring about us, but it was distressingly brief. You probably consider letters secondary to your articles, but I'm in urgent need of a long talk. Zeinab is well. She sends you her regards and reminds you of the medicine she'd asked you to get from one of your colleagues traveling abroad. I think her intestinal problems are simple, but she's fond of medicine, as you know. Buthayna is happy—how I wish I could read her mind—but the happiest of us all is certainly Jamila, who as yet understands nothing. You'd be amazed at the progress I've made—I've lost fifteen pounds, walked thousands of kilometers, sacrificed tons of meat, fish roe, butter, and eggs. Having stuffed myself to death for so long, I yearn for food. Since I find no one to talk to in your absence, I often talk to myself. Zeinab's speech is too sober, though why sober speech should annoy me these days I don't know. I met a madman on the road about a kilometer before the Glim beach. He assails those who pass by raising his hand in the manner of our leaders and delivering obscure speeches. He's the only one whose conversation I've enjoyed. He accosted me, saying, "Didn't I tell you?" I replied with concern, "Yes, indeed." "But what's the use? Tomorrow the city will be full of flounder and you won't find space for one foot." "The municipality should . . ." He interrupted me sharply. "The municipality won't do anything. They'll welcome it as an encouragement to tourism and it will increase to such fantastic proportions that the inhabitants will be forced to leave and the Agricultural Road will be packed with lines of emigrants and in spite of all this the price of fish will continue to rise. . . ."

I wish I could have read his mind, too. His language was no less strange than mathematical equations and we reasonable men are lost between the two. We who live in the corporeal, mundane realm know neither the pleasure of madness nor the marvels of equations. With all that, I remain the father of a happy family. Witness us as I confide in Buthayna while Jamila attacks us with sand. Our house in Glim is very comfortable. My craving for whiskey is increasing noticeably. Yesterday while we were in the beach cabin, we overheard our neighbor say that the apartment buildings would be nationalized. Zeinab blanched and looked at me, appealing for help, so I said, "We have a lot of money." She asked, "Can the money be rescued?" "We've taken out various insurance policies against fate." She began questioning me anxiously, "How do we know that . . . ?" But I interrupted her. "Then for God's sake how did you get so fat?" She exclaimed, "In your youth you were just like them. You talked about nothing but socialism, and it is still in your blood." Then she asked me again to remind you about the medicine. Mustapha, I don't care about anything. Nothing concerns me, honestly. I don't know what has happened to me. All that matters is that we resume our chats, our grand, meaningless chats. By chance I overheard a conversation between two lovers in the dark.

The man said, "Dear, it's becoming very dangerous." The woman replied, "This means you don't love me." "But you know very well that I love you." "You're speaking reasonably, which means that you no longer love me." "Can't you see I'm a grown man with responsibilities?" "Just say you don't love me anymore." "We'll destroy ourselves and our homes." "Will you stop preaching?" "You have your husband and daughter; I have my wife and children." "Didn't I say you don't love me anymore?" she said. "But I do love you." "Then don't remind me of anything but love."

I left imagining the delicious scandal and laughing at the woman's daring and the man's consternation. But they reminded me of an old friend called love. God, what a long time has passed without love! All that is left are mummified memories. How I'd like to sneak into the heart of a lover. As you know, Zeinab has been my only love; but that was more than twenty years ago, and what I remember of that affair are events and situations rather than the feelings and agitations. I remember I told you one day, "Her eyes slay me," but you never forsook me in my insanity. However, the memory of insanity is not like insanity itself—the feverish thoughts, volcanic heart, and sleepless nights. Agony lifted me to poetic ecstasies. Tears streamed from my eyes and I approached heaven. But these are no more than mummified memories. Here I am struggling to lose weight and I see in dear Zeinab only a statue of family unity and constructive work. Honestly, I've lost interest in everything. Let them take the three apartment buildings and the revenues. I won't claim that the principles which once nearly landed us in jail along with Othman make it easy to accept, for those days of strife are themselves no more than pallid memories. I don't know what has happened to me or changed me. Rejoice, dear friend, for while I grow healthy in body, I'm approaching an exquisite madness. May you be so lucky.

"Don't forget to write him about the medicine."

"I haven't, dear."

How sweet you are, Buthayna. Your budding breasts are proof of the world's good taste. Perhaps I'm an old conservative, for I've let your mother take over your instruction about the facts of life. It's regrettable that you know nothing about life, that I've kept you enclosed like a little canary in your school bus. What lies behind your dreamy look? Despite the frankness of our talks, haven't you withheld certain secrets from me? Are you affected by the scent of these bare bodies, by the flirtations exchanged among the waves? God, let society conform with her thoughts and deeds so that she won't be exposed to evil. He said to her as she was sitting with her bare legs stretched under his beach chair, "We haven't had such a good time together before."

"It's your fault."

"I've stayed in the office all my life for your sake alone."

She leaned back on her elbows, exposing her stomach and chest to the sun, which shone in the clear sky while one lonely white cloud floated above the curve of the bay. Her mother said without raising her head from her embroidery, "Tell him that his health is now more important than anything else."

"More important than the building nationalizations?"

She answered defiantly, "Even than the building nationalizations."

He remarked factually, "Social conformity is a fine thing."

She said nothing. A pretty girl strutted in front of them and the glance he caught from her delighted his senses like the scent of jasmine.

"When I return to normal, I'll have to develop a philosophy of life which allows true happiness."

"God help us."

"God wishes us to be concerned about the welfare of all." He glanced at her teasingly, then said, "But how would God respond to supplication in this case?"

She understood the implication, but withheld comment. He forgot the subject and turned to other thoughts. Although he felt lighter and more energetic, a nagging exasperation remained—the flies, his work, and his wife. One day Buthayna will be preoccupied by someone other than you, as will Jamila, who now builds pyramids in the sand. For God's sake, what do you want? Why does silence reign amid all the clamor? Why do you have the foreboding of fantastic perils? You hear the distressing sound of links snapping and feel that your footing is shaking so violently that your teeth will fall out. In the end you'll lose all your weight and float in space. Hold fast to things and regard them carefully, for soon their forms will disappear and no one will heed you. The waves are destroying Jamila's sand pyramid and the wind blows away the newspapers in which truth is relegated to the obituary sections. The client says to you, "I want to entrust my case to the Master." How ludicrous! Honorable counselors. All that's left for us is to work in the national circus.

"Why are you so distracted, dear?"

"It's nothing."

"Are you really all right?"

"I think so."

"Judging from experience, I think you're in need of care."

"We must respect experience."

"Shall I tell you the cook's opinion?"

"Does the cook have an opinion?"

"She said that the man who's satisfied and successful is vulnerable to the evil eye."

"And you believe that?"

"Of course not, but sometimes confusion drives us to seek any explanation."

"So all you have to do is consult an exorcist."

"Sarcasm was not in your nature before."

He said, smiling, "A little sarcasm doesn't do any harm."

"Let's forget it, dear."

On their way home, she detained him briefly as the two girls walked ahead. "I have some good news for you."

He looked at her with secret despair.

"I discovered something unexpected in Buthayna."

"Other than what you discovered last year?"

"Yes. She's a poet, Omar."

He raised his thick eyebrows in surprise.

"I'd noticed her absorption in writing and that she'd tear up what she'd worked on only to start it again. At last she confided to me that she writes poetry, so I laughed and told her. . . ."

Zeinab hesitated, so he asked, "What did you tell her?"

"I told her that you also started out as a poet."

He frowned and asked, "Didn't you tell her how I ended up?"

"But it's lovely for a girl her age to write poetry."

"It is."

"You must read her poetry and give her some advice."

"If my advice had any value it would have benefited me!"

"You're pleased with the news?"

"Very much so."

FOUR

His sudden happiness gave way to an agitation, alarming in its intensity, a feeling he had not known for the last twenty years. Buthayna, wearing a printed blouse and brown tapered pants, came at his beckoning to the balcony overlooking the sea.

"I wanted to invite you to watch the sunset with me," he said as she sat down in front of him.

She seemed on the verge of excusing herself, for, as he knew, this was the time she went out with her mother and sister for a late-afternoon stroll on the Corniche, so he said, "You'll join them soon. Poets should enjoy the sunset."

He noticed her cheeks redden, and smiled.

"But . . . but I'm not a poet!"

"But you write poetry."

"How do I know it's poetry?"

"I'll judge after looking at it."

"No," she said, timid and apprehensive.

"There's no secret between us. I'm proud of you."

"It's just silly scribblings."

"I'll love even your silly scribblings."

She lowered her eyes submissively, her long curving eyelashes nearly brushing her cheeks.

"Buthayna," he said with sudden concern, "tell me why you turned to poetry."

"I don't know."

"You do so well in science. What prompted you to turn to poetry?"

Frowning, she made an effort to remember. "The school readings. I enjoyed them very much, Papa."

"So do many people."

"I was more strongly affected, I think."

"Have you read any other poetry?"

"I've read some collections."

"Collections?"

She laughed. "I borrowed them from your library."

"Really?"

"And I know that you're a poet, too."

The remark pained him but he dissimulated gaiety. "No, no, I'm not a poet. It was a childhood pastime."

"You certainly were a poet. Anyway, I was strongly tempted by poetry."

You suggest the theater, my friend, but I'm a poet. I find myself caught in a whirlpool from which there's no escape except through poetry, for poetry is the very aim of my existence. Without it, what would we do with the love which surrounds us like air, the secret feelings which burn us like fire, the universe which oppresses us without mercy? Don't be supercilious about poetry, my friend.

"Tell me more."

She continued, regaining her usual courage. "It's as though I'm searching for tunes in the air."

"A nice sentiment, Buthayna, and poetry is fine as long as it doesn't spoil life. . . ."

"What do you mean, Papa?"

"I mean your studies and your future. But it is time to look at your poems."

She brought him a silver-colored notebook. With love and anxiety he opened the pages, but as he began to read, the year 1935 intervened tauntingly, that year of agony, secret schemes, wild hopes, and dreams of Utopia spurred by Othman's declaration that he had found the ideal solution. It was evident that his little girl, the bud which had not yet flowered, was in love. Who is this glorious being, whose breath is the clouds, whose mirror is the sun, and for whom the tree branches sway in yearning? Why should we be upset when our children travel the path we once took? What would his father think if he could hear him talking to his granddaughter about love?

"This is really poetry."

Her eyes shone with joy as she exclaimed, "Really?"

"Lovely poetry."

"You're only trying to encourage me, Papa."

"No, it's the truth." Then he asked her, smiling, "But who is he?"

The spark of enthusiasm died down in her eyes and she asked, rather disappointed, "Who?"

"Who is it you're addressing in these lyrics?" Then he said more forcefully, "Come, there are no secrets between us."

She answered enigmatically, "No one."

"It seems I'm no longer the father confidant."

"I mean it's not a human being."

"One of the angels?"

"Nor one of the angels."

"What is it, then—a dream—a symbol?"

In evident confusion, she replied, "Perhaps it is the final purpose of all things."

He wiped the perspiration from his forehead and arms and,

making a valiant effort to remove any trace of jest or sarcasm from his tone, said seriously, "Then you are enamored of the secret of existence."

She said nervously, "That's quite possible, Papa."

We're fools to think of ourselves as stranger than others. "And what brought all this about?"

"I don't know . . . It's difficult to say, but your poems first pointed the way."

Omar laughed mechanically, saying, "A family conspiracy! Your mother knew what you were up to all along and showed you that stuff which you call poetry."

"But it's wonderful poetry, and so inspired."

He laughed loudly, attracting the attention of the organ grinder below him on the Corniche who was filling the air with his jarring tunes.

"At last I've found an admirer! But it wasn't poetry, just a feverish delusion. Fortunately I got over it in time."

"While it makes me ecstatic!"

"So poetry is your beloved."

"As it is yours."

It was, but is no longer, and my heart feels the deprivation. Between the stars lie emptiness and darkness and millions of light-years.

"What is your advice, Papa?"

"All I can say is, do as you wish."

She asked gaily, "When will you take up poetry again?"

"For God's sake, let me get back to the office first!"

"I'm surprised that you could give it up so easily."

He said, smiling diffidently, "It was simply a frivolous . . ."

"But your collection of poems, Papa."

"I once thought I'd continue."

"I'm asking what made you stop."

He smiled sarcastically, but then a sudden desire to be frank prompted him to confess, "No one listened to my songs."

The silence hurt you, but Mustapha urged, "Perseverance and patience," and Othman said, "Write for the Revolution and you'll have thousands of listeners."

You were beset by privation and oppressed by the silence. Poetry could not sustain you. One day Mustapha announced happily that the Tali'a troupe had accepted his play. The silence became more oppressive. Samson fell asleep before he could destroy the temple.

Buthayna asked, "Do there have to be listeners, Papa?"

He reached over and stroked a lock of her black hair. "Why rescue the secret of existence from silence, only to be greeted by silence?" Then he added gently, "Don't you want people to listen to your poems?"

"Of course, but I'll keep on anyway."

"Fine, you're braver than your father, that's all."

"You can return to poetry if you want."

"The talent has died completely."

"I don't believe it. In my mind you will always be a poet."

What has poetry to do with this hulking body, with the preoccupation with legal cases, the construction of apartment buildings, and gluttony to the point of illness? Even Mustapha slumped on the couch one day as if he were declining visibly into old age.

"What wasted effort," he said.

You replied with concern, "But the Tali'a troupe welcomes your plays, and they're excellent works."

He gestured with his hand in deprecation. "I have to reconsider my life as you have."

"You've always counseled perseverance and patience."

He laughed harshly. "You can't ignore the public."

"You'd like to start out again as a lawyer?"

"Law died even before art. In fact, the concept of art changed without our realizing it. The era of art has ended, and the art of our age is simply diversion, the only art possible in an age of science. Science has taken over all fields except the circus."

"Really, we're all going to pieces, one after the other."

"Say rather that we've grown up, and regard your success in life as an exemplary case. I think that amusement is a splendid objective for the world-weary people of the twentieth century. What we consider real art is only the light coming from a star which died millions of years ago. So we'd better grow up and pay the clowns the respect they deserve."

"It seems to me that philosophy has destroyed art."

"Rather science has destroyed both philosophy and art. So let's amuse ourselves without reserve, with the innocence of children and the intelligence of men—light stories and raucous laughter and nonsensical pictures—and let's renounce delusions of grandeur, and the exalted throne of science, and be content with popular acclaim and the material rewards."

That both pleased me and saddened me. I suffered from conflicting emotions and recollected in dismay the one still in prison.

"Dear Baldy" applies the balsam of consolation to your failure with surprising skill. In the future he'll strive on a lower level for the force you once had. While you, who once searched for the secret of existence, have turned into a wealthy lawyer sinking in gluttony.

"If science is what you imagine, what are we but intruders on the periphery of life?"

"We're successful men with a secret burden of sorrow; it's unwise to open the wounds."

"We belong, in fact, to a bygone age."

"For God's sake, don't open the wounds."

"Scientists are strong through their allegiance to the truth, but our strength derives from money which loses its legality day by day."

"So I say that death represents the one true hope in human life."

Omar looked gently at his daughter's green eyes and said, "Buthayna, is it unreasonable to ask you not to give up your scientific studies?"

"No, I won't, but poetry will still be the most beautiful thing in my life."

"Let it be. I won't dispute that. But you can be a poet and at the same time an engineer, for example."

"You seem to be preoccupied with my future!"

"Of course! I don't want you to wake up one day to find yourself in the Stone Age while everyone around you is in the age of science."

"But poetry—"

He interrupted. "I won't contradict you, dear. My friend Mustapha finds poetry, religion, and philosophy in science, but I won't argue that position. I'm pleased and proud of you."

The large red disk of the sun was sinking, its force and vitality absorbed by the unknown. The eye could gaze easily at it now, as at the water. Rosy dunes of clouds pressed around it.

Do you really want to know my secret, Mustapha? In the agony of failure, I sought power, that evil which we'd wanted to abolish. But you already know this secret.

FIVE

In the fading glow of the sun, she looked sedate, even elegant. In spite of her extraordinary rotundity, the exasperating evidence of indulgence, she retained a winsome beauty. Her serious green eyes still had their charm, but they were now the eyes of a stranger. She was the wife of another man, the man of yesterday who hadn't known listlessness or fatigue, who had forgotten himself. How was she related to this man, the invalid without an illness, who avoided starches and liquor and who scrutinized the humid air for warnings of undefined peril? The two sisters are ahead; Jamila walks along the stone wall of the Corniche while Buthayna, on the street below, leads her by the hand. They are on the road between Glim and Sidi Bishr, where the crowds are a bit thinner. Buthayna attracted many glances and many murmured comments. Although indistinguishable, their meaning was clear enough. Omar smiled to himself. In a few years you'll be a grandfather, and life will go on, but where to? He watched the last of the sunset in the clear, pallid sky until only a sliver remained on the horizon.

He remarked, "The ancients used to ask where the sun disappeared to. We no longer question."

Zeinab looked at the sun for a moment, then said, "How marvelous to have ended the question!"

Rational answers strangle you to provocation. Sensible behavior annoys you unreasonably. How grand it would be if the sea turned violent, drove away those who loitered on the shore, incited the pedestrians on the Corniche to commit unimaginable follies, sent the casino flying above the clouds, and shattered the familiar images forever. So the heart throbs in the brain and the reptiles dance with the birds.

The two girls stopped in front of the San Stefano cinema, then resumed walking. Suddenly Zeinab put her arm through his and whispered imploringly, "Omar, what's wrong?"

He glanced with a smile at those around him. "So much flirtation!"

"That's nothing new. . . . What's wrong?"

He said, intent on ignoring her question, "There's a lot Buthayna doesn't know. I was thinking of that when I—"

She interrupted him impatiently. "I know what I'm doing. She's an unusually sensitive girl, but you're escaping."

Your soul longs for escape, the magic key at the bottom of a well.

"I'm escaping?"

"You know what I mean, so confess."

"To which crime?"

"That you're no longer yourself."

How we need a violent storm to wash away this cloying humidity.

"Only in body are you among us. Sometimes I'm so sad I could die."

"But as you can see, I'm following the regime rigorously."

"I'm wondering what's behind this change. Your behavior makes me question it again."

"But we diagnosed the condition thoroughly."

"Yes, but is there anything in particular which disturbs you?"

"Nothing."

"I must believe you."

"But apparently you don't, completely."

"I thought maybe something in your office or at the court had disturbed you. You're sensitive, but able to hide your feelings well."

"I went to the doctor only because I couldn't find a tangible cause."

"You haven't told me how it all started."

"I talked to you so often about that."

"Only about the results, but how precisely did it start?"

A reckless impulse drives you to confess. "It's difficult to establish when or how the change began, but I remember meeting with one of the litigants of Soliman Pasha's estate. The man said, 'I'm grateful, Counselor. You've grasped the details of the situation superbly. Your fame is well deserved. I have great hopes of winning the case.'

"I replied, 'So do I.' "

"He laughed contentedly and I felt a sudden, inexplicable wave of anger. 'Suppose you win the case today and possess the land only to have it confiscated tomorrow by the government?' He answered disparagingly, 'All that matters is that we win the case. Don't we live our lives knowing that our fate rests with God?' I had to admit the validity of his argument, but my head began to spin and everything seemed to disappear."

She glanced at him with surprise, and said, "That was the reason?"

"No, I don't know an exact reason, but I was undergoing a subtle, persistent change; thus I was agitated unreasonably by the man's words, words repeated by millions of others every day without any effect."

"Of course you can only think about death as men of wisdom do."

"I wonder how wise men regard death."

"Well, fortunately, that's known." She looked at him inquiringly. "And after that you hated work."

"No ... no, I can't say that. It may have been earlier, or later."

"I'm so depressed that I can hardly discuss it with you."

"Are you so concerned about the work?"

"I care only about you."

A case is postponed, another, then a third. You spend the day glued to your chair, legs stretched under the desk, chain smoking and staring vacantly at the ceiling.

"I'm tired of walking," she said.

"But generally you walk twice this distance."

She lowered her eyes. "It's my turn to confess. I may be pregnant."

His stomach sank and he yearned more sharply for the magic key of escape. "But," he murmured.

She said calmly, "Dear, God's will is stronger than any of our designs." Then she added, pressing his arm, "And you've not been blessed with your crown prince!"

As they walked back home, a coquettish smile played in her eyes. He said to himself that a bit of liquor would dissipate the languor so he could feign the role of lover, as he feigned marriage and health.

He woke up early, after a few hours of sleep, to the thudding of the waves in the dark, silent morning. Zeinab was sound asleep, satiated, her lips parted in a soft, steady snore and her hair disheveled. And you despair. It's as though you were doomed to thwart yourself. I don't love her anymore. After long years of love, shared life, and loyal memories, not a grain of love remains. Pray that it's just a symptom of the disease which will disappear with recovery, but now I don't love her. This is the most bitter disillusionment. You hear her snoring and feel no sympathy or tenderness. You look at her and only wonder what brought you together, who imposed this damned parody.

"Mustapha, there's the girl."

"The one leaving the church?"

"That's the one. She's wearing black in mourning for her uncle. How pretty she is."

"But her religion."

"I no longer care about those obstacles."

I told her how pleased I was that she'd condescended to meet me. In the public garden, Omar al-Hamzawi, the lawyer, had introduced himself, while she responded with a barely audible murmur, "Kamelia Fouad." Dearest, our love is stronger than all else. Nothing can stand in our way. She answered with a sigh, "I don't know."

Mustapha laughed at all the commotion, saying, "I've known you forever, and you've always sought trouble. A tempest at your house, a more violent one at hers. I'm spinning between the two."

Then what a marvelous attitude he'd had later when, raising his glass of whiskey, he'd said, "Congratulations to both of you. The past is buried, but she's sacrificed much more than you. Beliefs are apt to tyrannize even those who've deserted them. To your health, Zeinab. To yours, Omar."*

He took you aside and, completely drunk, began to expostulate. "Don't forget the bad times ahead, but never forget love. Remember that she has no other family in the world now. She's been cut from the tree, and has no one but you."

I married a woman of great vitality and charm, a model student of the nuns, refined to the letter. She seemed to be a born businesswoman, with an unflagging zeal for work and a shrewd eye for investment. In her era, you rose from nothing to great eminence and wealth, and in the warmth of her love, you found consolation for wasted effort, for failure, and for poetry.

Still sleeping, she rolled over on her face. Her nightgown slid up, exposing the naked lower half of her body. He slipped from the bed and went out to the balcony, shutting the door behind him. Enveloped by the murky air, he watched the waves racing madly toward the shore and the spray flying against the cabanas. Flocks of clouds had spread across the pale dome of the sky, fogging up the early-morning weather. No feet yet walked the ground. Your spirit was unreceptive and the air did not refresh you. How long will you wait for deliverance? If only he could ask Mustapha about the meaning of the contradictions. He's a great resource of ideas, even if he only sells popcorn and pumpkin seeds now. Does Zeinab have a role only after work? One of the waves rose to an extraordi-

*Kamelia converted to Islam and changed her name to that of the Prophet Mohammed's daughter, Zeinab. By marrying Omar, she also cut herself off from her family.

nary height, shattered in tons of foam, then spread out defeated, giving up the ghost.

Dear God, Zeinab and work are the same. This malady which turns me from work is what turns me from Zeinab, for she is the hidden force, she is its symbol. She is wealth, success, and finally illness. And because I'm sick of these things, I'm disgusted with myself, or rather because I'm disgusted with myself, all else sickens me. But who does Zeinab have apart from me? Last night was a bitter experience. Love shrank and withered, and all that remained was a quickening of the pulse, a rise in blood pressure, and stomach contractions chasing each other in a horrible loneliness; the loneliness of the wave absorbed by the sand, which never returns to the sea. She sings songs of love, while I'm mute; she's the pursuer while I'm the fugitive; she loves while I hate; she's pregnant while I'm sterile; she's sensitive, perspicacious while I'm stupid. She said you're unusually quiet. I said it's simply that my voice is unheard. I said, "Suppose you win the property settlement today and tomorrow the government confiscates the land?" to which he replied, "Don't we live our lives knowing that our fate rests with God?" Even in alienation, the wave rises insanely, shatters in foam, then gives up the ghost. The grave of sleep swallows you, but still you don't rest, your brain still chases phantoms. You even consider seeing the doctor again, admitting that you've changed unaccountably. What do I want, what am I after? Knowledge has no importance, neither have the legal affairs of my clients, the addition of a few hundred pounds to my account, the blessings of a happy home, and the reading of the daily headlines. So why not take a trip in space? Ride the light waves, for their speed is fixed, the only fixed thing in the constantly changing, insanely reeling universe.

The first spacemen have arrived, selling microbes, selling lies.

SIX

At the end of August, the family returned to Cairo. The view of Al-Azhar Square on his way to work the first day was upsetting. It remained a depressing thoroughfare, unchanged since his departure. He was warmly welcomed at the office, especially by Mahmoud Fahmi, his assistant, and the files were soon brought out, the postponed cases and those under review. September had its sticky days, but a gentle breeze had arisen and the early mornings were shaded by the suggestions of white clouds. Mustapha embraced him at length. They stood face to face, Omar towering above his friend, whose bald head, tilted back, was spotlighted by the silver lamp.

He said, sitting on the leather couch before the desk, "You're as slender as a gazelle. Bravo."

He took out a cigarette from the box—a wooden box ornamented with mother-of-pearl which played a tune when opened—lit it, then continued. "I often thought of visiting you in Alexandria, but family obligations called me to Ras el Bar. Apart from that, I was tied up in preparing a new radio serial."

Omar looked at the case files, then at his friend's eyes, pleading for an encouraging word. He smiled enigmatically, then finally said, "I worked without stop this morning."

Mustapha breathed a sigh of relief, but then Omar murmured, "But . . ."

Mustapha inquired anxiously, "But?"

"Honestly, I've regained no desire to work."

An uneasy silence prevailed. Mustapha exhaled the cigarette smoke with a tense expression, then suggested, "Maybe you should have taken more rest."

"Let's stop kidding ourselves. The problem is more serious than that."

Then he lit a cigarette in turn and continued to the echo of new tunes. "The problem is more serious, for it's not only work which has become unbearable. This illness is consuming other things, far more precious than work—my wife, for instance."

"Zeinab?"

He said with something like shame, "I don't know how to put it, but sadly enough, I can't bear her now. My house is no longer the happy abode."

"But Buthayna and Jamila are part of it."

"Fortunately they don't need me . . ."

Mustapha frowned and blinked his round, filmy eyes. In his inquisitive glance was a sorrowful, pressing desire to solve the riddle. "But someone of your intelligence can discover the secret."

He said, smiling bitterly, "Maybe the universe in its eternal, monotonous revolving is the primary cause."

"I'm sure you're exaggerating, at least as far as Zeinab is concerned."

"It's the appalling truth."

He asked with solicitude, "What's to happen in this state of affairs?"

"I live, questioning all the time, but with no answer."

49

"By now, you must be convinced, at least, that you're going through some sort of psychological crisis."

"Call it what you wish, but what is it, what do I want, what should I do?"

"You're too sensible to be plagued by questions. Probe your hidden desires, look into your dreams. There are things you want to run away from, but where to?"

"That's it. Where?"

"You must find the answer."

"Tell me, what makes *you* stick to work and marriage?"

Because the question seemed somehow funny, he smiled, but the sober atmosphere quickly dispelled his gaiety. "My attachment to my wife is based on reality and on habit. My work is a means of livelihood. Besides, I'm happy with my audience, I'm happy with the hundreds of letters I get from them each week. Acceptance by the public is gratifying, even if it means selling popcorn and watermelon seeds."

"I have neither public, nor reality, nor habit."

Mustapha paused a while and then said, "In fact, you've been extraordinarily successful in your work and your wife worships you, so you're left with nothing to fight for."

Omar smiled sarcastically. "Should I pray God for failure and adultery?"

"If it would help you regain some interest in life!"

Each retreated into himself and the tense silence carried ominous forebodings.

Omar spoke. "It sometimes consoles me that I hate myself just as much." He squashed his cigarette butt in the ashtray impatiently. "My work, Zeinab, and myself are really all one thing, and this is what I want to escape from."

Mustapha looked at him quizzically. "An old dream is enticing you?"

He hesitated before confiding, "Buthayna wrote some poems."

"Buthayna!"

"I read them, and while we were discussing them, I felt a strange yearning for the old books I'd deserted twenty years ago."

"Ah, how often I've thought that would happen."

"Hold on. Yes, a certain sensation crept into my sluggish brain and I began searching for lost tunes. I even asked myself whether it might be possible to start again. But it was just a fleeting sensation which soon disappeared."

"You retreated quickly."

"No. I went back to reading, and jotted down a few words, but it came to nothing. One evening when I was at the cinema, I saw a beautiful face and felt the same sensation."

"Is sensation what you're after?"

"Sensation or intoxication—the creature within me revived all at once and I believed it to be my aim, rather than work, family, or wealth. This strange, mysterious intoxication appeared as the sole victory among a series of defeats. It alone can vanquish doubt, apathy, and bitterness."

Mustapha looked at him steadily, his chin resting on his hand, and asked, "You wish to bid love a final farewell?"

He said, rather vexed, "So you think it's a symptom of middle age. However, this is easily cured when the respectable husband rushes off to the nightclub or marries a new wife. And maybe I, too, will run after a different woman. But what aggravates me is more serious than that."

Mustapha couldn't refrain from laughing. "Is it really a strange intoxication or simply a philosophical justification for adultery?" he asked.

"Don't laugh at me. You were once in a pretty bad way yourself."

A smile spread on his face as he looked into his memories. "Yes," he said, "I was starting to write a new play when suddenly I lost my grip. Art shattered in fragments, disintegrated into dust in my hands. So I exchanged it for another type of art, one which has given happiness to millions of our citizens."

"Well, I've missed the way. I turned from art to a profession which is also dying. Law and art both belong to the past. I can't master the new art, as you have done, and like you, I failed to study science. How can I find the lost ecstasy of creation? Life is short and I can't forget the vertigo caused by the fellow's words: 'Don't we live our lives knowing that our fate rests with God?' "

"Does the idea of death disturb you?"

"No, but it urges me to taste the secret of life."

"As you found it in the movie theater?"

He doesn't know of your walks through the streets and squares of Alexandria, yearning for a face which promised the long-sought ecstasy, of your lingering under the trees by the stream which swayed with the cries of your burning emotions. The mad giant searching for his lost mind beneath the damp grass.

He referred to these times at some length, speaking with a solemnity befitting the mysterious and strange. "Those nights I was not an animal moved by lust, but I was suffering and in despair."

SEVEN

*"I can't help wanting you more every time we meet.
The flame leaps higher with each heartbeat."*

"A passionate song. Who's the singer?"

"Margaret. The star of the New Paris."

The crescent-shaped garden which bordered the dance floor was cooled by the autumn breeze. The music came from a stage set inside red walls and lit from within.

"She looks English."

"That's what the owner of the nightclub claims, but what passes for English in the nightclubs could easily be something else."

The fine lines of her face, a certain look in her eyes, the lightness of her movement—perhaps it was the harmony of all these which evoked something of the long-sought ecstasy.

"I envy your expertise in these forbidden pleasures."

"Just part of my job as editor of the magazine's art section!"

"Bravo ... You said her name is Margaret."

He answered laughing, "Or twenty pounds a night, not counting the liquor."

The gentle autumn breeze carried greetings from an unknown world, a world not inhabited by just one mind, a world whose four corners lay behind the darkness of the cypress trees.

"I'm in a mood where anything could happen."

"But don't drink more than one glass!"

"The first thing is to invite her to the table."

Mustapha went to look for the waiter. The fragrance of lilies spread in the air, and in the intervals of silence, the whispering of the branches was audible. He was eager to enter his life of fantasy. Strange shapes of human beings passed before his eyes and he said to himself in apology that all this was the effect of illness.

Margaret approached the table, swaying in her dark evening gown, and greeted them with a smile which displayed her perfect set of teeth. The waiter, her shadow, stood a few feet away.

"Champagne," Omar ordered.

You first drank it on your wedding night. It was a cheap brand, a joint present from Mustapha and Othman. What would the prisoners do if struck with an epidemic of your strange disease?

Mustapha's greeting indicated that he had known the woman previously. "Margaret," he said, "we both admired your voice, and my friend is quite taken with you. It seems that every time you meet . . ." He winked, laughing. "He's a prominent lawyer, but I hope you won't need him in any professional capacity."

Her mouth spread in a soundless laugh, and she said, "I always need someone to defend me. Isn't that the case with women in general?"

Omar summoned forth a gift for flattery which had lain dormant for many years. "Except for those with your beauty and voice."

Mustapha said, with a cunning blink of his filmy eyes, "He

started out as a poet, you know, but he hasn't yet reached the standard of 'I can't help wanting you more.'"

Inspecting Omar, Margaret said cautiously, "A poet . . . but he looks so sedate!"

Omar responded, "That's why I gave it up so quickly."

"So now he regards beauty as a treatment which will cure him of the strange illness he's been suffering from recently."

The champagne bottle popped open and the bubbles raced into their glasses.

"That means I'm some sort of medicine?"

Mustapha followed quickly with a smile. "Yes, why not, of the sort that one takes before sleep."

"Don't rush things. The cure doesn't come as easily as you think."

Omar asked her to dance. Out on the floor, with his arm around her waist and the fragrance of her perfume quickening his senses, he savored the night. The humidity had relented, and the trees, alight with red and white lamps, seemed to have bloomed.

"May it be a happy acquaintance."

"You're as charming as you are tall."

"You're not short yourself."

"But your sharp eyes frighten me."

"They're shining only from joy, but I'm not much of a dancer. I've almost forgotten how."

"Don't you see you're too tall to be a good dancer?"

"When my friend invited me to the New Paris he said I'd like what I'd find."

"Really."

Lying comes so easily in the autumn. Mustapha was clapping for them as they returned to their seats. Omar's face glowed with a boyish happiness, and for a moment, bewitched by the night's charms, he was restored to his lost youth. She touched the ring of his left hand, murmuring, "Married . . . really, you married men don't give the bachelors a chance."

Mustapha said, laughing, "You two are getting along famously. I bet you'll go out together tonight."

"You've lost the bet."

"Why, my dear Margaret? A lawyer like our friend won't tolerate delay."

"Then he must learn."

"Conventions be damned!"

Omar said gently, "In any case, my car's at your disposal to take you wherever you'd like."

When she got into the car with him, he was elated. "Where to?"

"Athens Hotel."

"Have you seen the pyramids after midnight?"

"It's a dark night without any moon."

He headed in the direction of the pyramids. "Civilization has robbed us of the beauty of darkness."

"But—"

He said reassuringly, "I'm a lawyer, not a playboy, or a highway bandit."

His heart had not stirred like this since the rendezvous in the Jardin des Familles. He could hardly remember Zeinab's youthful face and hadn't really looked at their wedding picture for the past ten years. You, Margaret, are everything and nothing. With the desperation of a fugitive, I knock at the gate of the enchanted city.

"Under this open sky by the pyramids, great events took place."

She lifted his arm from around her neck, saying, "Please don't add to those events."

He pressed her hand in gratitude nonetheless.

"It's best that we don't stop," she said. "Don't you see how strong the wind is?"

"We're well protected inside."

How dense the darkness is around us. If only its density could shut out the world, obliterating everything before the weary eye so that the heart alone might see, might gaze on the blazing star of ecstasy. It approaches now like the rays of dawn. Your soul seems to shun everything in its thirst for love, in its love for love, in its yearning for the first ecstasy of creation and for a refuge in the wellsprings of life.

"Why don't we spend the night here?"

"Be sensible. Please take me back."

"You've never heard of what goes on at night at the pyramids?"

"Tell me about it tomorrow."

He leaned toward her and they exchanged a kiss; but then she restrained him, pleading, "I said tomorrow."

He kissed her cheek lightly, signaling retreat, and started moving the car over the sand.

"Please don't be angry."

"I yield to the eternal conditions."

"Eternal?"

"I mean the feminine conditions."

"Actually, I'm tired."

"So am I, but I'll arrange the right place for us."

"Wait till we meet again."

"I'll start setting things up."

"Wait a little."

"I have a feeling that we'll stay together."

"Yes," she said, looking ahead at the road.

It was nearly dawn when he returned home, and as he rode the elevator, he remembered how his father used to rebuke him for his late-night escapades. Entering the bedroom, he saw Zeinab sitting on the dresser stool, looking at him with dulled and saddened eyes.

He said quietly, "You should have been asleep."

She spread her hands in despair. "This is the third night."

Undressing, he said distantly, "It was unavoidable."

She asked him more sharply, "Home upsets you?"

"No, but it's true, I am disturbed."

"And how have you spent your nights?"

"No place in particular, at the movies, at coffeehouses, roaming around in the car."

"And I'm here with all kinds of ideas running through my head."

"While you should be sound asleep."

"I'll grow ill in the end."

"Follow my advice."

She sighed deeply. "You treat me with such deadly coldness."

There's no doubt of that. The man you know has shed his skin and now he runs panting after a mysterious call, leaving behind him a trail of dust, all the joys of yesterday, all his Utopian dreams, even the girl whose youthful beauty held such promise in store when church bells rang. Infatuated, you

once looked into those green eyes and said, "Love is fear-
less."

She murmured, clinging to you, "But my family."

"I'm your family, I'm your world. The Day of Judgment
will come before I desert you."

Today your life hangs on a cheap song.

Sleep, Zeinab, for your sake and for mine.

Another woman stood on the red stage, singing,

> *"I can't help wanting you more every time we meet.*
> *The flame leaps higher with each heartbeat."*

He leaned over to Mustapha. "Where's Margaret?" he
asked.

Mustapha got up to inquire, then returned saying, "An unpleasant surprise."

"What is it?"

"She's gone."

"Where?"

"Abroad."

"Did this happen unexpectedly?"

Mustapha brushed his hand disdainfully. "Let's look for
someone else."

EIGHT

This act of faithlessness set off a reaction twice as intense and he felt he was in a desperate race with insanity. In the end those swaying branches would speak. Mustapha asked, "Do you really think this is the remedy?"

"Maybe. It's the only thing that's helped so far."

He stopped the car in front of the Capri Club and said as they were getting out, "I've tried so many things, as you know, to no avail. I did feel a heartthrob with Margaret. Passing illusion that she was, the heartthrob was real."

They sat under a trellis roofing. In the dim light, the people sitting at the other tables appeared to be phantoms.

Mustapha remarked, "The manager of this club is a friend of yours," and indicated a man standing at the far end of the stage. He was a short barrel of a man, with a fleshy white face and heavy jowls puffed up like a waterskin. His heavy-lidded eyes peered drowsily yet they had a certain mischievous tilt. When he saw Mustapha he moved toward them with surprising speed for one so heavy. Omar recognized him as a former client for whom he'd won two cases. The man shook their hands warmly, then sat down, saying, "Omar Bey, this is a pleasant surprise." He ordered whiskey and went on. "I never dreamed you'd stop by here, but after all, those who work hard deserve to play."

Mustapha interrupted with a decisive voice. "Let's dispense with the formalities, Mr. Yazbeck." As the manager looked at them warily, Mustapha laughed. "It's as you suspected. The time has come to return the good services of your lawyer."

"Omar Bey?"

"I thought of asking you to recommend a suitable girl for him."

The man smiled broadly and said, "A refined and beautiful girl . . . of good family."

"I'm speaking about love, not marriage!"

"It's up to him, sir."

"Do you have any such cultivated lovelies?"

He waved his small, soft hand in deprecation and said proudly, "Capri's main attraction."

He went on to elaborate, still glancing at Omar a bit skeptically. "She was a student at the Drama Institute, but wasn't a success at acting. She loves to dance, though, and has created a sensation at the Capri."

"Warda!"

"None other."

Mustapha said apologetically, "I didn't think of her because of her height, which would naturally discourage me."

Yazbeck gestured grandiosely toward the stage, where the musicians had started playing an Oriental dance. A storm of applause greeted the dancer, a magnificent statuesque woman with wide-set languid eyes and a high forehead which gave her face a certain aristocratic distinction.

Mustapha murmured, "Marvelous."

Yazbeck said jestingly, "You're immune to such delightful temptations . . ."

"I'm self-sufficient. It's a pastime enjoyed by the best of husbands."

Omar smiled, remembering how Mustapha once said that he couldn't betray his wife since he wasn't able to make love with anyone else. Then he drifted away from the voices around him as he followed the movements of the lovely body, lithe in spite of her height. He loved her smile as he loved the cypress tree. Yazbeck's outstretched hand, bidding them goodbye, drew him back to awareness. After the man had gone, Mustapha looked at him seriously and cautioned, "The raptures of love are seldom found in nightclubs."

Omar muttered sarcastically, "He who strives will be rewarded."

"You know whenever I see Zeinab now my conscience bothers me."

He said scornfully, "These pains are more severe than the luxury of conscience."

Mustapha pointed out the problems involved in such affairs, but Omar interjected, "In the feminine sex, I seem to see life on two feet."

Warda walked directly toward them, without pretense of delay, her wide, gray eyes glancing steadily at Omar. The scent of the jasmine flowers she wore in her bracelet diffused in the air. Shaking his hand, she exclaimed happily, "At last I've found a man I don't have to look at from above!"

She sat down between the two men and flicked her hand so that the jasmine spilled onto the red tablecloth. The champagne came and bubbled forth. Warda seemed composed, but there was a look in her gray eyes that cautioned against haste. She exchanged a smile of familiarity with Mustapha and listened to the accustomed praise of her dancing and beauty. Throughout, she continued looking at Omar with respect, while he searched her gray eyes for some clue, some answer to his unsatisfied longings. I came not because I loved but in order to love. The complexion is clear, the scent pleasant, and the long eyelashes alluring.

"So you're the famous lawyer?"

"That's of little importance unless you have problems."

"My problems can't be solved through the law courts, unfortunately."

"Why unfortunately?"

"They might have been solved by you."

Mustapha said, laughing, "He's trustworthy, both in court and outside it."

He noticed her long neck surrounded by a simple pearl strand, the bare spread of her chest, the healthy passion expressed in her full, colored lips and flowing from her eyes, and felt his being throb with a strange and unbounded desire, like the mysterious yearnings which assailed him in the late hours of the night. He wished to address the depths, and to have the depths speak to him without an intermediary, but if the long-sought ecstasy eluded him, he would find a substitute in the firebrand of sex, the convulsive climax which consumes the wine of life and all its dreams in one gulp. He was delirious with longing, anticipation, the titillation of adventure, the effect of abandoned drinking, the scent of jasmine pressed under his glass, Warda's encouraging glance, a star blinking through a gap in the trellis. As the club showed signs of closing, he said, "Shall we go?"

Mustapha said his farewells and left.

Warda was impressed by the sight of his Cadillac, an elegant little coupe de ville. "Where's your home?" he asked.

"It's out of the question. Don't you have a place?"

"With a wife and two daughters."

"Then take me home as those without homes do."

He drove out to the desert by the pyramids, racing madly, seeking the shelter of the open sky as he had with Margaret. The half-moon was sinking toward the west. He reached toward her and gave her a light, artful kiss as a start. Then they exchanged a long kiss, incited by passions as old as the moon.

She sighed, whispering. "This is nice."

He pressed her against him with a fervor which stretched into the solitudes of the desert. His fingers entwined in her hair, which was lit by moonbeams, and he said in a strange, breathless voice, "When the dawn comes."

With his cheek pressed against hers, they gazed at the sleepy moon, on a level with their eyes, and followed its languid beams on the sand. Its beams would die, leaving the heart still thirsting. No power on earth can preserve this godly moment, a moment which has conferred a secret meaning to the universe. You stand on its threshold, with your hand stretched out imploringly toward the darkness, the horizon, and the depths where the moon has fallen. A firebrand seems to burn in your chest as the dawn breaks forth and fears of bankruptcy and want recede.

"Are you a dreamer?" she asked.

"No, I'm realistic to the point of illness."

She laughed. "But you're not a woman beater."

"I don't beat men either."

"That's good."

Pressing her closer, he said, "But at one time, I was about to kill."

"Because of a woman?"

"No."

"Don't talk of such things in the moonlight."

"In the end I decided to kill myself."

"In my presence?"

"In your arms."

"In the moonlight?"

"Now the moon is disappearing."

When he returned home and switched on the bedroom light, Zeinab opened her lifeless eyes. As he greeted her indifferently, she said tensely, "It's almost dawn."

"So?"

She sat on the bed, her eyelids swollen, looking tormented and desperate.

"I haven't heard this tone from you in all the years we've been married."

He put on his pajamas in silence and she cried out, "I've never heard anything like it."

He muttered resignedly, "Illness is like that."

"How can I bear such a life?"

"My days are spoiled. Don't spoil the nights."

"The girls are asking questions."

"Well, let's face the situation with a certain amount of wisdom."

She buried her face against the wall. "If only I had some place to go."

He turned off the light and lay down, closing his eyes. Soon, the first movements of the morning would be heard, and tears would be shed next to him, while betrayal gnawed beneath like an insect. Only a few moments remained before this existence would die. She's cut off from the tree and no longer has anyone but you. It's strange that you should be filled with such determination. Tonight's ecstasy is as erratic as a bolt of lightning. How can it fill the emptiness of life?

On Friday he sought out Buthayna on the balcony while she was watering the flowerpots. He smiled somewhat bashfully, but she welcomed him by racing over and presenting her cheek to be kissed. In spite of her happy glow, he detected in her evasive glance a faint reprimand.

"I've missed you very much," she said.

He bit the inside of his lip and said, "I'm sorry, but I'm determined to get well, and just need a bit of forbearance."

She turned back to the flowerpots, and he asked, "Are you okay?"

"Yes," she said, then added after a pause, "But Mama's not."

"That's understandable. But things will change. Just be patient."

She pointed out a jasmine bud, still barely visible, and exclaimed happily, "The first jasmine. It's very small but the scent is strong. Shall I pick it for you?"

NINE

How strange it seems, going to work every day in an office which had become so alien and meaningless. When would he have the courage to close it down?

The head clerk remarked, "Every day we lose another case. I've become almost inactive."

In fact, he'd left the burden of work almost entirely to others and did very little supervising or reviewing anymore. Gloomy eyes stared at him from the walls in the stagnant, musty air. His creative energies were spent outside now in setting up the flat in Soliman Pasha Square.

"I'm glad we're setting up our own place," he said to Warda. "We can't go to the pyramids in winter."

She asked, swinging her shoulders to a jazz beat under the trellis of the Capri, "When winter comes, will you still be interested in our affair?"

He raised his glass of champagne. "To a permanent affair." Yazbeck was standing in the distance, the grand master of ceremonies. Omar returned his smile and said, taking Warda's hand, "I owe a lot to him."

"He's nice and better than most of his sort, but greedy, as you'd expect."

"But I'm a champagne customer."

She frowned slightly. "It's extravagant to come here every night."

He beamed, murmuring, "Your concern is encouraging."

She embraced him with her eyes, and said, "Haven't the pyramids already witnessed that?"

"Yes, love, and for me it's not just an affair as I said, but ..."

She urged silence with a press of her hand. "Don't name it. Isn't it better that it names itself?"

"You're so lovely, it drives me mad."

"I have no confidence in words, since I was originally an actress."

"And a lady through and through."

"Thank you, but you know most people have a low opinion of the art. For that reason I left my family. It's just as well I have no brother or father."

He thought for a moment, then said, "Certainly acting would be better than dancing at the Capri."

"I didn't have the proper devotion to it, and they said I had no talent. Dancing was my real love all along, so it was the Capri, and the rest followed, inevitably...."

He said with warmth, "But you have a heart of gold."

"That I've never heard before."

He commissioned a couple of men to work on the new flat—the furniture, the bar, the objets d'art and decor. And soon the place was quite beautifully set up. Apart from the bedroom, dining room, and entrance hall, there was an Oriental room which recaptured the fantasies of *A Thousand and One Nights*. He spent without limit, as though ridding himself of a painful financial tumor. He followed Mustapha's amazed eyes as he toured the place, and when they finally met his glance, said, "Instead of reprimanding me, talk to me about the meaning of life."

"Life!"

"I'll knock the deaf walls at every spot until the voice inside betrays the hidden treasure."

Mustapha shrugged resignedly and said, "There is a certain beauty in the madness."

"The last few days have given me a taste for life I've never had before. Nothing else matters."

Mustapha said, smiling, "Yazbeck's uneasiness proves the girl's loyalty."

"She's loyal and honest or else the greatest of actresses."

"But she's a failure as an actress."

The apartment overwhelmed her when she entered it the first time. She exclaimed in admiration, "You really do have champagne taste, but you've been too extravagant."

He gave her a light kiss and said, "This is our little nest."

"I don't want to burden you or give you any false impressions about me."

"If I didn't know the real Warda, I wouldn't have made any effort."

She laughed coquettishly. "You're alone responsible for your understanding."

"And the pyramids?"

"Just because we shriek when fire burns us doesn't mean shrieking is in our nature."

He stretched out on the divan, saying, "Mustapha tells me Yazbeck is upset."

"I refused to go out with anyone else. He can jump in the lake."

"And stay there indefinitely."

"I'll restrict my work at the Capri to dancing."

"You're so sweet."

"It's hot today. I'm going to take a shower in the new bathroom."

He changed from his street clothes into a galabiya, for that, he decided, was more in keeping with the Oriental room than pajamas. Looking contentedly around the elegant place, he reflected that happiness was enough to cure him; he could let up on the regime. A sudden lightheartedness prompted him to ask in a booming voice, "What's the shower water up to?"

Her voice responded behind the bathroom door, "Something very impolite!" The door opened, she darted past him, wrapped in a towel, and shot into the bedroom. He closed his eyes in contentment. May this nest repeat the ecstasies of the pyramids, and what he now holds in his hands, may it satisfy her longings. For its sake he has tread on other hearts and learned recklessness and cruelty. May she not vanish as Margaret did. Your colleague, the great lawyer, said to you in your office, "You look too dapper these days for a successful, hardworking lawyer."

You laughed. "Less so for a happy lawyer."

He glanced at him with misgiving, the brazen lover, then quickly changed the conversation to politics, his favorite subject. "So, what are people doing these days?" he asked.

Uninterested in politics, you answered, "Searching madly for ecstasy."

He didn't understand. He's a womanizer, but you're not. You're neither brazen nor frivolous, but who distinguishes between the slayer and the worshipper, or believes you're building a temple from the wreckage?

The bedroom door opened halfway, and her head appeared. "Making up is tedious. I'm dying for a kiss."

He rushed over to her and held her cheeks between his hands, pressing her mouth closed, and as he kissed her, he savored the fragrance of her soap, the scent of her skin. "Shall I come in?" he whispered.

Laughing, she pushed him away and said, "Don't be primitive."

He reclined again on the divan, and looked at the radio-television console in front of him. In a playful mood, he got up and turned both of them on at once and was assaulted by a discussion of juvenile crimes running simultaneously with "Listener's Request." He turned them off, but still feeling playful, went to the bedroom door and knocked. "Hi," the voice called.

"I love you."

"With all my heart."

"What do you want most in life?"

"Love."

He continued in a playful tone. "Have you ever thought of the meaning of life?"

"It has no meaning apart from love."

"Have you finished making yourself up?"

"Just a minute more."

He persisted. "Doesn't it bother you, love, that we play while the world around us is serious?"

She laughed exuberantly. "Don't you see that it's we who are serious while the world around us plays?"

"Where do you get such eloquence?"

"After a while you'll learn the secret."

When the night is spent and the relentless dawn overtakes us, you'll return inevitably to the dreary room where there is no music, no ecstasy, where sad eyes and a wall of stone will close upon you. Then the chords of somber wisdom will ring out with reproaches as harsh as the dust of a sandstorm. Make your reply as resolute and final as your aversion.

"Don't disturb me." Deafen your ears to all words. "I said, don't disturb me. This is the way I am, today, tomorrow, and every day.... Accept matters as they are, and leave our daughter out of the quarrel." "There is no point in arguing, I'll do as I please." And don't back down if Buthayna asks why you've changed. "Think what you want, I'm too bored by it all to make excuses."

The door opened and Warda emerged in all her splendor. "What do you think of me, sweetheart?"

He looked at her dazzled, and murmured, "Let me be a sentence never uttered by a tongue before."

TEN

She sat facing him on the balcony that Friday, their holiday, and he reflected uneasily that he'd hardly seen her the past week. The rays of the sun crossed her lap and her legs and sparkled on the Nile beneath them. It was strange that he couldn't remember her as a child, whether she was a devil like Jamila. Now she's a beautiful girl, intelligent, studious, refined, poetic. Her resemblance to her mother as a girl he preferred to forget.

"You're too serious for a poet!"

Jamila, who'd been standing at the entrance to the balcony, shouted defiantly, "A poet!"

He shook his finger at her, then turned to Buthayna, whose serious expression showed signs of displeasure. "You're too thin, and your sister's too fat. What do the two of you eat?"

Jamila shouted, "She eats."

Umm Mohammed, the maid, carried off the protesting Jamila.

"Mama's unwell," Buthayna said.

"Mama's all right. Tell me about you."

"There's nothing much to say, but Mama's not all right."

The chase never stops in this house. And you, Buthayna, does nothing concern you but poetry, math, and chemistry? Is God alone your lover?

"You don't like to talk about Mama?"

"She no longer understands my illness."

Their eyes met for a moment; then, defeated, he turned to look at the Nile.

"But the doctor, Papa."

He interrupted her gently, trying to hide his exasperation. "I'm the doctor, no one else."

"I'm sorry, but you've taught me to be open with you."

"Of course."

Suddenly a shrill little voice shouted, "Course!" He held the little girl's arm until Umm Mohammed took her away again.

"Have we caused you irritation?"

"God forbid. But we tend to escape when we're disturbed within ourselves."

"She cries a lot and that's very painful."

"You must convince her that she's mistaken."

She said, playing with the bracelet of her gold watch, "But you treat her differently now. You told her very harshly you'd do as you pleased."

"She told you that, too?"

"I'm the only one she can complain to."

Depressed, he muttered, "It was just anger, as you know."

"Anyway, she's willing to help you as much as she can."

"There's nothing she can do."

She hesitated a moment, then said, "Mightn't she think . . ."

"Isn't it better for us to go over your latest poems?"

"There's nothing new."

"But your lover still inspires you."

"Maybe she thinks . . . well, you know."

"She even lets you in on her ridiculous fears."

"It makes me very sad."

Lighting a cigarette, he said, "Ridiculous illusions."

She said anxiously, "I'll believe you. You've always been a model of truth. Are they merely illusions?"

You're backed into a corner. "Your mother has upset you too much."

"Say that they're just illusions."

He glanced at her reproachfully, but she avoided his eyes. Looking at the Nile, she asked, "There's no other woman?"

"A woman!" the shrill little voice returned.

This time he pulled her onto his lap as though seeking her protection and started roughhousing with her, the only way to deal with the little imp. But Buthayna continued her worrying. "I want an answer, Papa."

"What do you think of your father?"

"I believe you, so speak. Please, for my sake, speak."

In bitter despair, he said, "There's nothing."

Her face brightened while his heart sank. Her eyes shone with victorious relief but the world scowled. Autumn was in the air, a tinge of yellow had spread over the treetops, and flocks of white clouds were reflected in the gray water. The emptiness was filled with silent tunes, sad and delicate, and weary questions with hard answers. His lie expanded until it threatened him with annihilation.

In the depths of despair, he went to visit Mustapha at his office. After a futile discussion, Mustapha concluded, "I've gone along with you and helped, hoping that you'd realize the futility of this venture, but you're drowned."

He sighed. "You don't realize I'm living the art I always longed to create."

Mustapha finished the page he was writing, then sent it down to the press. "I've often thought the crisis you're suffering resulted from suppressed art."

He rejected the idea with a shake of his head, then said, "No, it's not art, but it may be what we turn to art in search of."

Mustapha paused a minute, then said, "If we were scientists, spending twenty years of our lives searching for an equation, perhaps we'd be invulnerable to despair."

Shaking his head sorrowfully, he said, "My misfortune may be that I'm searching for an equation without scientific qualifications."

Mustapha laughed. "And since there's no revelation in our age, people like you can only go begging."

Begging, day and night in aimless reading, in futile poetry, in pagan prayers in the nightclub halls, in stirring the deaf heart through infernal adventures.

Mustapha spoke about Zeinab and said that she was suffering, both from his desertion and from the effects of her pregnancy. She must be in a bad way. You've become so hard-hearted, yet you're prepared to be magnanimous if she'd only free you from the shackles of this dead love.

"Yes, Zeinab, there is another woman, since you insist on knowing."

Disgust has sprouted in a fetid swamp choked with traditional platitudes and household management. What wealth and success you've attained offer no comfort, for all is consumed by decay. Your soul is sealed in a putrid jar like an aborted fetus, your heart suffocated by apathy and by grimy ashes. The flowers of life, withered and fallen, will come to rest on the garbage heap.

"Weep all you like, you'll have to accept things as they are."

Disaffection has killed everything. A few questions have

tumbled the very foundations of life. I said to him, "Suppose you win the case today and the government confiscates your land tomorrow?" to which he replied, "Don't we live our lives knowing that our fate rests with God?"

He was in his office, dawdling over a memorandum, when the office boy announced Mr. Yazbeck. The man walked in, his paunch bulging in front of him, greeted Omar with a bow, and sat down.

"Since I was passing through Al-Azhar Square, I thought I'd drop by for a visit."

Omar said with a sarcastic smile, "You'd come from the far ends of the earth for Warda's sake, wouldn't you?"

"My dear counselor, you know that my garden is full of roses."

"Fine, so don't talk about Warda."

He smiled broadly and said, "It would be foolish to think I could get around you, but let's try to bridge the distance between us as directly as possible."

"Yes?"

His eyelids lowered and he said seriously, "Warda's been neglecting her duties."

"She has duties other than dancing?"

"You didn't honor us with your presence that night, sir, just to watch Warda dance."

"So?"

"So I said I'd complain to the great man himself."

Omar frowned but remained silent. Yazbeck continued. "Business is business, sir, and I don't like . . ."

He interrupted curtly. "Do whatever you think is in your interest."

"I don't want to anger you . . ."

"But I'm excusing you in advance."

The man bowed his head gratefully. "And I promise I'll take her back to work if you tire of her in the future."

"That day will never come, Mr. Yazbeck."

"I wish you happiness, *mon chéri*."

Yazbeck was about to get up, but Omar, overcome by a sudden absurd impulse, detained him. "Tell me, Mr. Yazbeck, what meaning does life hold for you?"

The man raised his eyebrows in surprise, then, reading the seriousness of Omar's expression, answered, "Life is life. . . ."

"Are you happy?"

"Praise the Lord. . . . Sometimes business is slow, sometimes the club is disturbed by a love affair like Warda's, but the carnival goes on. . . ."

"So you live knowing your fate rests with God?"

"That's undeniable, of course. But I have a beautiful house, a good wife, a son studying chemistry in Switzerland who's going to settle there."

He smiled. "Do you believe in God?"

The man replied in astonishment, "Naturally. What an odd question."

"Then tell me what He is."

He laughed openly, for the strange questions had removed all ceremony. "Will your infatuation for Warda last long?"

"Of course."

"Couldn't it . . . ?"

He interrupted. "If you tell me what God is, I promise I'll let you have her immediately!"

The man rose, bowed once more, and said on his way out, "I'm always at your service."

ELEVEN

He kissed her with fervent gratitude. "I know it's a great sacrifice to quit your job."

Her wide eyes shone with tears. "For your sake."

The Oriental room exuded the breath of love. He'd never dreamed he would love her so intensely. She withdrew a dark blue box from the pocket of her robe and handed it to him shyly—a gift of golden cuff links.

He exclaimed, as though he'd never owned gold before, "Sweetheart!"

"The cuff links, you can see, have two hearts."

"Because your heart is made of gold, as I told you."

Running her fingers through his thick black hair, she asked, "Why did you bring all your clothes with you today?"

His face clouded, and he said in a voice devoid of tenderness, "I've left home for good."

She exclaimed in astonishment, "No!"

"It's the only solution."

"But I told you, I don't want to cause you any trouble."

"Let's not talk about it."

The room's atmosphere in the silence of dawn was electric. She looked at him with angry and desperate eyes, her makeup smudged with all the tears she'd shed. How ravaged by anger is a face which had remained placid for twenty years.

"You should train yourself to accept the facts."

"While you stain your honor with a prostitute."

"Your voice will wake everyone up."

"Look at the lipstick on your handkerchief. How disgusting!"

Overcome by anger, he shouted, "What of it?"

"Your daughter is of marriageable age."

"I'm ridding myself of death."

"Aren't you ashamed? I'm ashamed for you."

His anger increasing, he replied, "Accepting death is even more shameful."

Her head dropped as she wept. "Twenty years without knowing your filth," she said in a choked voice.

He said insanely, "So, let it be the end."

"I'll wander around aimlessly."

"No, this is your home; so stay. I'll go."

You threw yourself on a chair in the living room, your eyes closed with pain. Hearing a noise, you raised your head and found Buthayna standing before you, pale-faced and still drowsy-eyed with sleep.

The atmosphere was charged with guilt and reproach as you gazed at each other in silence. You remembered the disgraceful lie, and in all your life had never felt so ashamed.

"I'm sorry, Buthayna, for upsetting you."

The compressed lips revealed her wounded pride. "There's no use in talking," she said, then reverted to silence, succumbing to the burden which had fallen upon her.

"Your mother will remain in the house, provided with every comfort."

He prayed to God that she wouldn't cry. "It's distressing," he murmured, "but I'm ridding my soul of something more serious."

She looked sadly into his eyes. "But you told me there was nothing."

His face burning, he sighed. "The truth was inappropriate."

"Why?"

"Let's preserve what love there is between us."

You left, unable to meet her glance again until she pardons you.

Warda commented, "You'll regret your decision."

"No, I can't stand the hypocrisy anymore."

She said anxiously, "I'm so afraid that I'll fail to make you happy."

"But I am happy, really."

And so he applied himself to happiness and shunned all disturbing thoughts. Anticipating resistance from Mustapha, he accosted him. "I'm happy. Does that displease you? I even feel some poetic stirrings."

He also became more receptive to work, though he was still reluctant to accept cases. His work breaks were spent talking to her on the phone, and at the end of the day, he would rush back to his nest and she would welcome him with a shining face. They usually stayed in the Oriental room, but sometimes they'd go out to the distant parts of Cairo, to the rendezvous of lovers; sometimes they'd take night excursions to Fayum or to the rest house on the Desert Road. When she learned that his poetical aspirations of the past were again seeking expression, she encouraged him with superb recitations of her own. As a student at the Drama Institute, she'd memorized Shawki's plays, and many love poems as well.

He said to her admiringly, "Your love of poetry is wonderful."

She urged him to start writing again, but he was reluctant. "Isn't it better to live poetry than to write it?"

One day she remarked, "You haven't asked me about my past."

Giving her a kiss, he answered, "When we're in love, we accept everything on faith. There's no need to ask questions."

But she wanted to talk about her past. "My father was an English teacher, a wonderful teacher, the sort that students never forget. If he'd been alive when I decided to enter the Drama Institute, he would have given me his blessings and encouragement. But my mother's a very pious, narrow-minded woman. I entered the Institute against her wishes, and when I decided to take up dancing, she was furious. So were my uncles, on both sides. It ended in our cutting off relations. I deserted my family."

"And how did you manage on your own?"

"I lived in the house of one of my actress friends."

He fondled her soft hand and asked, "Have you always loved dancing?"

"Yes, I loved to dance, but I had aspirations of being an actress. I tried, and failed, and so ended up as I started, as a dancer."

He asked, disturbed, "Did Yazbeck bully you?"

"Actually, he's kinder than the others, and I knew what working in a nightclub entailed."

"You're my first and last love," he said fervently, pressing her to him in gratitude. Then he asked, "Why didn't you return to your mother after you'd failed in acting?"

"It was too late. I have my pride, and failure only intensified it."

Failure! The curse that never ends. It's awful that no one

listens to your songs, that your love for the secret of existence dies, so that existence itself loses all mystery. Sighs of lament will one day destroy everything.

The office witnessed sober visits from his uncle, a justice, and from his only sister. They besought him not to marry "the dancer" and his uncle observed, "If this relationship continues, you won't be considered for the justiceship."

He said rather abruptly, "I haven't striven for it or wanted it."

He defended his happiness fiercely, with all the force of despair which had seized him. He seemed so childishly gay and innocent that Mustapha remarked, laughing, "Now tell us about the meaning of life."

Omar laughed loudly. "That question nags at us only when our hearts are empty. . . . A full vessel doesn't produce hollow sounds. Ecstasy is fulfillment, so I can only hope that love will bring everlasting ecstasy."

"Sometimes I pity you, other times I envy you." Omar's eyes shone triumphantly as Mustapha continued. "As fast as I speed through life, now and then the old sense of failure, buried deep in my heart, returns—perhaps on one of the dusty days of the sandstorm season, and I'm bedeviled by questions about life's meaning, but I soon repress them, like shameful memories."

A wintry wind rattled the windows of the office and the late afternoon faded into night. Mustapha's bald head would now brave the cold. He went on. "Why do we ask? Religious conviction provided meaning. Now we try to fill the void with the verifications of natural law. Yesterday, frustrated and dissatisfied, I asserted that my artistic commentaries were meaningful, that my past and present radio programs were meaningful, that my television plays were meaningful, and so I had no right to question."

"What a hero you are!"

He continued enumerating his achievements. "The way I made love to my wife last night was so fantastic that I suggested to the editor that it be written up as 'The Artistic Event of the Week.' My son Omar, unfortunately named after you, has become a sulky adolescent, as mad about soccer as we once were about overturning the world."

He overturned the world and landed in jail. But someday he'd get out, in a few years, and astonished glances would be exchanged. Let others worry about it.

Mustapha remarked in a more serious vein, "The editor suggested that I give a lecture to the employees on socialist consciousness."

"In what capacity?"

"In my capacity as an old socialist!"

"You accepted, of course?"

"Of course, but I wonder, with the state so intent on applying its progressive ideals, isn't it better for us to be concerned with our own private affairs?"

"Such as selling popcorn and watermelon seeds and wondering about the meaning of life?"

"Or falling in love to find the ecstasy of fulfillment."

"Or growing ill without cause."

They smoked in silence, then Omar asked suddenly, "How are they?"

Mustapha smiled. "Zeinab is fine, back to normal, though exhausted by her pregnancy. But there's something you should know."

Omar showed signs of interest.

"She's thinking of looking for work after the delivery."

He made a gesture of annoyance as Mustapha continued. "As a translator, for example. I'm afraid that she'll leave home one day."

"But it's her home."

Mustapha looked at him sarcastically. "Buthayna's immersed in her studies, and Jamila has almost forgotten you."

He lowered his eyes, disconcerted.

"And I fulfill my duty by criticizing you relentlessly in the bitterest terms."

Omar laughed. "You old hypocrite."

"My wife, on her part, never ceases attacking you."

"Of course, of course."

"I often defend you when we're alone and attribute your behavior to a 'severe psychological illness,' reassuring her at the same time that it's not infectious!"

TWELVE

No one excelled Warda in the art of love. Mad about her man and their little nest, she devoted herself completely to the service of love and to performing all its tasks. Omar would look around the place, smell the roses in the vase, listen to the music in the Oriental room, and would feel he was in paradise. Though she asked nothing of him, he would urge her occasionally to buy clothes and other things. She tried to keep her weight down by taking walks and watching her diet, and urged him also to be careful about his eating and drinking. He felt that she'd become a part of his personality and that she clung to him as her last hope. In the long winter nights they withdrew into themselves and stayed in the Oriental room until late at night, and between kisses and embraces talked endlessly about the past, present, and future, about truth and fantasy, reality and dreams, and were it not for the closed porch overlooking the square, the winter storms and rain showers would never have disturbed them at all. When conversation was exhausted, the silence that fell was one of mutual understanding, security, and comfort. But at times he was overcome by his fantasies, some of them laughable, others more disturbing. He was alarmed by one particular vision: the collision of two cars at a crossroad, a middle-aged gentleman tossed in the air.

"Where are you?" the gentle voice whispered.

He answered, a bit ashamed, "It's nothing."

She put her arm around his neck. "It must be something important."

He shook his head. After a moment's silence she probed again. "Why wouldn't Buthayna and Jamila visit you in your office?"

He was thinking of what a strange house the spider builds to hunt flies. "Buthayna didn't want to."

"She knew of your wish?"

"Mustapha conveyed it to her."

"You haven't talked to me about it."

"It's not important."

"Whatever concerns you is important to me."

They began to watch television more. It helped in fore-stalling the strange fantasies. Mustapha rang them up one day to ask how they were. She invited him to drop by, and so he began visiting them. He asked Omar how his poetry was progressing.

"He does write," Warda replied.

Omar protested, "It's an abortion."

"Happiness is more important than poetry," Mustapha said consolingly.

He was on the verge of asking, "But what is happiness?" but the concern, so evident in Mustapha's gray eyes, deterred him. Mustapha and the radio and the television rescued them from repetitious talk. And then there were his fantasies, "Oh God!" He saw himself as a magician, entertaining the people with his miraculous powers. He would cause the opera house to vanish in the blink of an eye, as the astonished crowds looked on, and then, to exclamations of wonder, suddenly restore it. Dear God, how much we need such potions of magic. As he gazed at her dreamily, she asked, "Why don't you invite some friends over to pass the time?"

He said quietly, "I have no friends besides Mustapha."

She seemed unconvinced, so he explained, "I don't consider colleagues and acquaintances friends."

So she arranged, on her own, for them to go out more often, to the theater and the cinema, even to the nightclubs.

"Isn't this better," she said, "than staying alone by ourselves at home?"

He nodded in agreement.

She reproached him. "This is the first time you've been unflattering!"

Too late, he tried to make amends. "I simply meant to compliment you for arranging these outings."

"I'll never tire of your company."

"Nor I of yours, believe me."

He was annoyed at his inattentiveness. Dear God, what's happening? Mustapha, at any rate, was clearly impressed by his happiness, and remarked one day as they were sitting together in his office, "Tell me about love. In the end you may persuade me to adopt a new philosophy of life."

Omar saw the glint of maliciousness in his eyes. Ignoring the question, he asked, "Have I become so unimportant to Buthayna?"

"You know she's idealistic and proud, but in her heart she adores you."

"Hasn't she missed me, the traitor?"

"She'll see you again one day, but for God's sake tell me about this romance of yours."

"As strong as ever!" he said defiantly.

"A political declaration?"

"You have no right to probe the secrets of the heart, you hypocrite!"

Mustapha laughed at length, and said, "Let me describe the situation as I see it. Those delightful conversations are dwindling, the games are losing their charm, inadvertently you drink more."

"Drop dead."

How awful. Warda was the perfect lover and beautiful as well. Dear God, how can ecstasy be aroused again and the dead poetry revived? How dark the late afternoon of winter.

They went one night to the New Paris and suddenly Margaret appeared on the stage. His heart raced, remembering the past, but with a great effort of will, he controlled his nerves.

She sang:

"I can't help wanting you more every time we meet.
The flame leaps higher with each heartbeat."

Warda whispered, "How true."

One glance exchanged between you and Margaret would be a giveaway. So they left at his suggestion, and drove aimlessly in the cold night through the empty roads. There's no need to be agitated, no reason to be. But her sudden return gave impetus to his vexation. You'll stand at the edge of the abyss again, prey to the forces of destruction summoned forth by despair.

He called Warda from the office to tell her he'd been invited to a party in honor of a colleague recently appointed justice. He went to the New Paris and listened to Margaret sing while he waited. What brought me here, and why so quickly? What am I looking for? Is it all over with Warda?

Margaret came to the table, along with the champagne. Her face glowing, she said, "I'm sorry I had to leave so unexpectedly."

"Unexpectedly?"

"I received a cable from abroad."

He studied her, marveling at the force of her attraction. He asked her to leave with him, but she answered, "Not tonight."

He tried to control his impatience. "When?"

"Perhaps tomorrow."

When he returned to the nest, around one o'clock that night, Warda was sitting in the Oriental room. He kissed her and asked, as he'd once asked Zeinab, "You're still awake?"

She said reprovingly, "Of course!"

She looked at him for a while, then remarked, "I hope you haven't overeaten or drunk too much."

Later as he was lying in his pajamas on the couch, she crept over to him and pressed her lips to his, but he felt no stirrings of desire. "Let it be an innocent night," he said to himself.

She called him at work the next day, but unable to think of any excuse, he made no mention of his plans to be absent. He went off to the New Paris congratulating himself on his indifference. The red lights transformed Margaret into a bewitching she-devil, and her slender neck and rich voice thrilled him.

Spanish lamps hung from a ceiling covered with paintings of nude women. How can ecstasy filter into such a place, filled with cigarette smoke and the odor of wine? Peering behind a huge pillar, he saw a couple embracing as if in the throes of death.

Could Warda be uprooted so easily from his soul, as if only an artificial flower? Why are we reminded of death so insistently, whatever we do? Who can affirm that these drunken souls really exist?

They raced out to the pyramids in his car. "The night's cold," she objected. He turned on the heater, but she kept on. "Why don't we go to your home?"

"I have no home."

He stopped the car in the darkness. A heavy bank of clouds covered the sky. "Not a star in sight," he said happily.

He pressed her to his chest with desperate force. She whispered breathlessly, "The darkness is frightening."

He silenced her with a kiss, then said, "Now is not the time for fear."

How wonderful her touch was, yet in itself it meant nothing. To touch life's secrets is all that matters. Their words were lost in sighs, the silent language of the night; a song of harmony seemed to herald a better life, and their intermingled breaths warmed a heart stricken with cold. The darkness was free of peering eyes. The heart could relax and rejoice triumphantly. He sighed with the fullness of pleasure, he sighed with relaxation, but then, dear God, he sighed with weariness and distress. He looked into the black night and wondered where ecstasy was. Where had Margaret gone?

He returned to the nest discontented. She faced him with rigid features, he smiled in greeting, and they remained standing for an uncomfortable minute. Then he flung himself on the couch, saying, "I'm sorry."

"There is no need to invent excuses." She walked back and forth across the room, and then sat in a chair near him.

"It's been clear to me that you've needed a change."

"Things aren't that simple."

Unable to control her anxiety, she said, "I'm not going to conduct a cross-examination. Just one simple question. Have we failed?"

He answered truthfully, but wearily. "No one can match you. I'm sure of that."

She looked off into space. "Were you with a woman?"

He hesitated a moment before answering, "To tell you the truth, I'm not yet cured of the illness."

She spoke sharply for the first time. "An illness whose only cure is a woman!" Then she resumed her calm tone. "All I can offer you is love, so if you refuse it, all will end." She observed his silence with a kind of desperation, and then went on. "Fickle passions in the young can be cured; in wise men like you they can't."

His eyes wandered hopelessly around the room. "Am I insane?"

"Oddly enough, your personality doesn't seem unstable."

"But I'm accused of insanity because of my behavior."

She burst out, "If you mean living with me, then go back to your wife."

"I have no wife."

"Then I'll go. My situation's easier than your wife's since I can always get a job and a place to stay."

Her words stung him, almost causing him to shout, "Go!" but instead he stretched out his legs and closed his eyes.

"So you were with a woman?"

He answered with annoyance, "You know."

"Who?"

"A woman."

"But who is she?"

"It doesn't matter."

"You knew her before knowing me?"

"We'd met casually."

"Do you love her?"

"No."

"Then why did you go out with her?"

He shrugged.

"Maybe you felt a sudden desire?"

"Maybe."

"Do you always give in to your desire?"

"Not always."

"When?"

He was getting vexed. "When I feel ill."

"Are you a womanizer?"

"No."

"Weren't you in love with me?"

"Yes, certainly."

"But no longer?"

"I love you, but the illness is starting again."

She said impatiently, "I've been noticing a change in you for the last few days."

"Since the illness set in."

"The illness ... the illness!" she shouted with exasperation, then asked, her expression distorted, "Are you going to meet her again?"

"I don't know."

"Do you enjoy torturing me?"

He blew out a breath. "A rest break, please."

He took Margaret one cold, starry night to the rest house on the Desert Road, and on the way back she said tenderly, "Wouldn't it be better to have a place of our own?"

"No ..." he said vaguely, having decided there was no point in continuing with her.

Displeased with his answer, she said coldly, "I really don't enjoy affairs in parked cars."

He drove her back to the hotel without saying another word.

THIRTEEN

The ecstasy of love fades and the frenzy of sex is too ephemeral to have any effect. What can we do when we find no food to satisfy our hunger? You'll be swept into the tornado and annihilated. There is no way to bring back stability after it has died.

A brunette dancer at the New Paris attracted him with her gaiety and lithe body, so he went after her. He saw Margaret on the stage, returned her smile, then invited the brunette to his table. To Margaret it must have seemed a clumsy ploy in the game of love, but in the storm he'd lost all sense of humor. The brunette left with him, enticed by money. It didn't really make things better, but he thought his heart stirred slightly as she laughed. If his heart didn't stir, it would die. Poetry, wine, love—none of them could call forth the elusive ecstasy.

Every night he picked up a woman, from one club or another, sometimes from the streets. At the Capri he sat with a dancer called Muna. Yazbeck rushed over to greet him, exhibiting obvious pleasure. It angered Omar, for he saw it as a kind of death notice of his frustrated hopes.

"My good man. Did . . . ?"

Omar looked at him sternly and left with Muna. As he pressed her to him, he trembled with an unaccountable urge to kill her. He imagined himself ripping open her chest with a knife, and suddenly finding what he'd been looking for all along. Killing is the complement of creation, the completion of the silent, mysterious cycle.

"What's wrong?" Muna whispered.

He awoke, startled. "Nothing, just the dark."

"But there's no one around."

He raced the car at such a speed that she grasped his arm and threatened to scream. Later, as he was undressing, he felt that the end was coming—the answer to his search—insanity or death. Warda sat on the bed. "I'm going away," she said.

He answered gently, "I feel responsible for you."

"I don't want anything." After a moment's silence, she spoke again. "What's sad is that I've really loved you."

He said wearily, "But you're not patient with me."

"My patience is at an end."

He felt such revulsion toward her in his soul that he didn't comment.

Finding no trace of her when he returned the next night, he smiled in relief and lay down in his suit on the divan to enjoy the silent, empty flat. Every night he brought a new woman to it.

Mustapha laughed and said, "Hail to the greatest Don Juan on the African continent."

Omar smiled lamely as Mustapha continued. "It's no secret anymore. Several of my colleagues have spoken about you. The news has also reached your cronies at the club. They wonder what's the story behind your rejuvenation."

He said with distaste, "Honestly, I hate women."

"That's obvious!" Then he continued more seriously. "Empty your heart of what's troubling you so you can settle down, once and for all."

In the spring it was a relief to sit outdoors in the nightclub gardens, rather than in the closed halls. But the agitation remained, and he was exhausted by his dreams. Occasionally he found solace in reading, especially the poems of India and Persia.

His nighttime adventures took him once more to the Capri. As he sat under the trellis, sipping his drink and receiving the spring breeze, Warda appeared again on the stage. He felt no emotion, surprise, agitation, or pleasure. In autumn it had started. Ecstasy, love, then aversion; when will the grieved heart smash these vicious cycles? When will it break through the barrier of no return? She sees him, then continues dancing, while Yazbeck steals worried glances. He felt no determination. But after the show, noticing Warda not far from him, he invited her to his table. She approached with a smile, as though nothing had happened. He ordered the usual—the drink which had earned him renown in the clubs—and said with sincerity, "I'm really sorry, Warda."

Smiling enigmatically, she said, "You shouldn't regret what has passed." Then gaily: "And the experience of love is precious even if it brings suffering."

He said, biting his lip, "I'm not well."

She whispered, "Then let's pray to God for your recovery."

He felt the glances of the other women who'd gone with him, night after night. As Warda smiled, he muttered, "I didn't desire them."

She raised her eyebrows.

"I knew them all, without exception, but there was never any desire."

"Then why?"

97

"Hoping the divine moment would unlock the answer."

She said resentfully, "How cruel you were. You men don't believe in love unless we disbelieve in it."

"Perhaps, but that's not my problem."

The scent of orange blossoms drifting from the dark fields suggested secret worlds of delight. Feeling suddenly light and unfettered, he asked her fervently, "Tell me, Warda, why do you live?"

She shrugged her shoulders and finished her drink, but when he repeated the question, he was so clearly in earnest that she replied, "Does that question have any meaning?"

"It doesn't hurt to ask it once in a while."

"I live, that's all."

"I'm waiting for a better answer."

She thought a moment, then said, "I love to dance, and to be admired, and I hope to find true love."

"To you, then, life means love."

"Why not?"

"After loving once, weren't you disillusioned?"

She said with annoyance, "That may be true of others."

"And as for you?"

"No."

"How many times have you loved?"

"I told you once . . ."

He interrupted her. "What you told me once doesn't matter; let's discuss things openly now."

"Your violent nature is getting the better of you."

"Don't you want to talk?"

"I've said all that I . . ."

He sighed, then continued feverishly. "And God, what do you think of Him?"

She looked at him distrustfully, but he entreated, "Please answer me, Warda."

"I believe in Him."

"With certainty?"

"Of course."

"How does such certainty arise?"

"It exists, that's all."

"Do you think about Him often?"

Her laugh was a bit forced. "When in need or adversity."

"And other than that?"

She said sharply, "You love to torture others, don't you?"

He stayed in the club till 3 A.M. and then raced out in the car to the Pyramids Road. Going out alone that night, he reflected, was an interesting development. He parked the car along the side of the deserted road and got out. The darkness, unrelieved by ground lights, was peculiarly dense, unlike any night he could remember. The earth and space itself seemed to have disappeared and he was lost in blackness. Raising his head to the gigantic dome overhead, he was assaulted by thousands of stars, alone, in clusters, and in constellations. A gentle breeze blew, dry and refreshing, harmonizing the parts of the universe. The desert sands, clothed in darkness, hid the whispers, as numberless as the grains, of past generations—their hopes, their suffering, and all their last questions. There's no pain without a cause, something told him, and somewhere this enchanted, ephemeral moment will endure. Here I am, beseeching the silence to utter, for if that happened, all would change. If only the sands would loosen their hidden powers, and liberate me from this oppressive impotence. What prevents me from shouting, knowing that no echo will reverberate? He leaned against the car and gazed for a long time at the horizon.

Slowly it changed as the darkness relented and a line appeared, diffusing a strange luminosity like a fragrance or a secret. Then it grew more pronounced, sending forth waves of light and splendor. His heart danced with an intoxicated joy, and his fears and miseries were swept away. His eyes seemed drawn out of their very sockets by the marvelous light, but he kept his head raised with unyielding determination. A delirious, entrancing happiness overwhelmed him, a dance of joy which embraced all earth's creatures. All his limbs were alive, all his senses intoxicated. Doubts, fears, and hardships were buried. He was shadowed by a strange, heavy certitude, one of peace and contentment, and a sense of confidence, never felt before, that he would achieve what he wanted. But he was raised above all desire, the earth fell beneath him like a handful of dust, and he wanted nothing. I don't ask for health, peace, security, glory, or old age. Let the end come now, for this is my best moment.

The delirium had left him panting, his body twisted crazily toward the horizon. He took a deep breath, as if trying to regain his strength after a stiff race, and felt a creeping sensation from afar, from the depths of his being, pulling him earthward. He tried to fight it, or delay it, but in vain. It was as deep-rooted as fate, as sly as a fox, as ironic as death. He revived with a sigh to the waves of sadness and the laughing lights.

He returned to the car and drove off. Looking at the road dispiritedly, he said, as if addressing someone else, "This is ecstasy." He paused before continuing. "Certainly, without argumentation or logic." Then in a more forceful voice: "Breaths of the unknown, whispers of the secret." Accelerating the car, he asked, "Isn't it worth giving up everything for its sake?"

FOURTEEN

The ringing of the telephone in the empty nest awakened him. He picked up the receiver and heard Mustapha's voice. "Where were you all night?" When he didn't answer, the voice went on. "Zeinab has gone to the hospital."

There was a moment of incomprehension before he recalled that he was a husband, and a father with more of fatherhood in store. In the waiting room he found Buthayna, Mustapha, and Aliyyat, his wife, a staid, strong-willed matron in her forties, on the short side, plump, and with a round face and features. When it was Buthayna's turn to greet him, she held out her hand with lowered eyes, to hide her agitation.

"She's in the delivery room," Mustapha said, "and everything is going normally."

As he was about to enter, Aliyyat detained him. "I was just with her, and I'm going in again right now."

"Shouldn't I go in too?"

Mustapha said, "It's better to avoid any sudden excitement."

It was only a short while before Aliyyat returned and with a beaming face announced to Omar, "Congratulations. You've got your crown prince and Zeinab is being taken to her room."

He sat down beside Buthayna, looking at her tenderly, and placed his hand on hers without a word. In her shyness she let it rest there for a while, then gently withdrew it.

Mustapha followed these motions, and said, "Fortunately hospitals are places where feuds are buried."

Hiding his disappointment at the withdrawal of her hand, he asked, "When did she get here?"

"Around midnight."

While he and Warda, animated by champagne, were having their discussion.

"And you didn't go to school?"

"Of course not, she came with her mother."

"Thank you, Aliyyat, thank you very much."

"You're welcome," she said, leaving for Zeinab's room.

"By dawn, she was very tired," Mustapha remarked.

Ah, dawn in the desert and the glimpse of a perfect, eternal ecstasy. But where is it? Mustapha excused himself to go catch some sleep. The two of them, he and Buthayna, remained waiting. Sensitive to the awkwardness of the situation, he said in a conciliatory tone, "You haven't slept, Buthayna?"

She shook her head, looking at the beige carpet in the hall.

"Don't you want to talk to me?"

Fearful of a showdown, she asked, "What can I say?"

"Anything. Whatever is on your mind. I'm your father and your friend. Our relationship cannot be severed."

She remained silent, obviously touched.

"Don't we agree about that?"

She nodded, and her lips moved in assent.

"You're angry, which is understandable. But whatever the problem is, it doesn't affect you directly. Your alienation from me is unbearable. I've invited you to visit me repeatedly. Why have you never come?"

"I couldn't."

"Did anyone prevent you?"

"No, but I was so sad."

"Was your sadness greater than our love?"

She said bitterly, "You never once came to see us."

"That wasn't possible. But you should have come when I repeated the invitation so often. Your refusal only made matters worse."

She tried to steel herself against the tears that were threatening. "Grief prevented me."

"That's too bad. Passivity is a trait I don't like, and I needed you after I'd left." Then he smiled to ease the tension of the situation, and said, "Enough. There's no time for reprimands now." He patted her shoulder and asked, "How's the poetry?"

She smiled freely for the first time.

He said enthusiastically, "You know we may be closer to each other today than we've ever been before."

"What do you mean?"

"It seems we're both drawn to the same source."

She turned her green eyes to him, seeking clarification.

"I've been reading poetry again and have been trying my hand at it."

"Really?"

"Abortive attempts."

"Why is that?"

"I don't know. Maybe the dust is too thick to be shaken off at once. Maybe the crisis resists poetry."

"The crisis?"

"I mean my illness."

She smiled, looking at the ground.

"Don't you believe me?"

"I always believe you."

Her words cut him, but he said, "You must believe me, in

spite of that one lie. It was a necessary lie, but it will never be repeated. My illness is real."

"You haven't yet discovered what it is?"

He thought a moment, then said, "Suffering—the only cure is patience."

She said compassionately, "Which you don't find with us?"

He stated quietly, "I'm living alone."

She looked at him with astonishment.

"Alone, believe me."

"But . . ."

"Alone now."

She responded with an urgency which gratified him. "Why haven't you come back, Papa?"

He kissed her flushed cheek. "Maybe it's best to remain this way."

"No." She held his hand and repeated, "No."

Aliyyat returned to tell him he could see Zeinab. As he entered the room, he saw her lying in bed covered from the neck down with a white sheet. Her face was very pale, drained of vitality, and her eyes were half closed. He felt sympathy, respect, and a certain regret. Here she is, able to create, while all his efforts have failed. He murmured in embarrassment, "Thank God, it all went well."

She smiled faintly.

"Congratulations. You've produced a crown prince."

He sat there, feeling awkward, until rescued by the arrival of Aliyyat and Buthayna. Aliyyat helped relieve the tension with her jokes and anecdotes, and after a while the baby was wheeled in on his cot. They uncovered his face, a red ball of flesh with rubbery features. It was hard to believe it would ever fall into shape, let alone an acceptable one. But he was reassured by his previous experiences of fatherhood—indeed, the subject of one of them was leaning over the cot right now, her green eyes peering at the baby with amazement and tenderness. He felt nothing in particular toward the baby but knew that he would grow to love him as he should. The child's neutral, rather startled look was enough for the moment. If you'd been able to express yourself, I would have asked you about your feelings, and your memories of the world from which you've just come.

"Have you chosen a name for him?" asked Aliyyat.

"Samir," Buthayna answered.

Samir, the companion and entertainer. May his name protect him from grief.

Aliyyat said pointedly, "Let's hope his upbringing will be in the hands of both parents."

He'd glided along the brink of creation, yet there was no intimation of change. He felt as alienated as ever. The newborn child had not bridged the gap between Zeinab and himself. He began wondering how long he'd have to sit there, the object of their glances and curiosity.

As lunchtime approached, he took his leave. Buthayna followed him outside, and her usual openness with him was apparent as she said, "Papa, you won't remain alone . . ."

He really didn't need the empty flat anymore now that he was dreaming of a new kind of solitude. "What do you want?" he asked submissively.

"I want you to come back."

Kissing her cheek, he said, "On condition that you won't get fed up with me."

Her face beaming, she took his arm and walked with him to the outer door.

FIFTEEN

He returned home, unchanged, feeling neither love nor hatred for Zeinab. But the disappearance of hatred signified the disappearance of Zeinab herself, the victory of his advancing exile over her world.

"We must accept this ordeal courageously," he told her.

And indeed she appeared brave, even deserting his bed. Touched by her attitude, he commended her. "You're a model of patience."

He refrained from his futile night adventures, and was able to find pleasure in his children. But as he watched the Nile flowing incessantly under the balcony, he yearned for the peace of that desert dawn. He spent his nights in his room, reading and meditating, then at daybreak he would return to the balcony, look at the horizon, and wonder: Where is peace? The poems of the Arabs, the Persians, and the Indians are full of secrets, but where is happiness? Why do you feel so depressed within these patient walls, why this uneasy feeling that you're only a guest, soon to depart?

"Thank God," Mustapha said. "Everything is back to normal."

He replied angrily, "Nothing is back to normal."

Mustapha avoided arguing out of kindness, but Omar would not let up. "I have not returned home; I have not returned to work."

"But, my dear friend . . ."

"And no one knows what changes the next hour has in store."

One afternoon the door of his office opened suddenly and a man entered. He was of medium stature, with a shaved head and a large, pale face. His nose and hands were strong, and his amber eyes had a sharp glint. Omar looked at him incredulously for a moment, then stood up and exclaimed in a trembling voice, "Othman Khalil!"

They embraced and then sat down facing each other on the two chairs in front of the desk. Unable to control his excitement, Omar kept on repeating his greetings, congratulations, and blessings, while Othman smiled, as though he didn't know what to say. Then there was a short pause and they exchanged glances. Fantasies mingled with memory, but in the depths of his being Omar felt a certain misgiving, a certain premonition of fear. So often he'd envisioned the meeting and had dealt with it in his imagination, yet it had now come as a surprise. He'd lost track of time and everything else recently—he knew that the prison term would not have ended yet, but hadn't realized that three-quarters of it had already passed. In his present psychological state, he was not ready for the meeting. A man reenters this world from prison; another man leaves this world for an unknown universe.

"It's been such a long time."

Othman smiled.

"You were never absent for an hour from our minds. And here you are, determined to live a normal life again."

He said in a rich, guttural voice, "You haven't changed in appearance, but your health is not up to par."

Omar was pleased that he'd noticed. "Yes, I've suffered a

strange crisis. But, please, let's not talk about me. I want to listen to what you have to say."

Othman waited until the servant had brought in a Coca-Cola and a coffee, then said, "Years and years have passed. The day is as detestable as the year; the year as trivial as the day. But I'm not going to reminisce about prison life."

"I understand, I'm sorry . . . but when did you get out?"

"Two weeks ago."

"Why haven't you come before now?"

"I went straight to the village, where I came down with influenza. When I recovered, I returned to Cairo."

There's no use in trying to escape. Your sense of guilt increases by the moment. "It tortured us that we couldn't visit you."

Othman said with an expressionless face, "Any visitors other than family members would have been arrested."

"We longed for reassurance about you."

"We were badly treated in the beginning, but after the Revolution, of course, things changed."

Omar winced.

"If we were thrown into hell, I believe we'd get used to it eventually and to its fiery minions."

He yielded to his sense of guilt. "It would have been more just if we'd gone with you to jail."

Othman said sarcastically, "It was the law, not justice, which threw me in jail."

He murmured submissively, "In any case, we owe you our freedom, perhaps even our lives."

"Wouldn't you have done the same thing if you'd been arrested and I'd gotten away?"

Embarrassed and ashamed, Omar remained silent.

Othman continued bitterly. "Here I am, back in the world again in my mid-fifties."

Omar tried to console him. "You're still young and have a long life ahead of you."

"And behind me an experience more bitter than despair."

He said sadly, "We lived outside the bars without, I'm afraid, accomplishing anything important."

Othman protested, "Don't say that. Don't rob me of my only consolation."

The sense of dread returned, and a feeling that he was a corpse, lying forgotten on the earth's surface.

"We practiced our professions, married, had children, but I feel I have nothing to reap but dust. You must excuse me, I have no right to talk about myself."

"But we are two integral halves."

The past is over, and the reckoning is hard. Othman had boasted in the basement of Mustapha al-Minyawi's house, "Our cell is an unbreakable fist of iron. We work for humanity as a whole, not for one country alone. We propose a human nation, a world of tomorrow founded on revolution and science."

After he'd been chosen by lot, he'd said, "I'm glad. Mustapha's nervous and you're a newlywed. Tomorrow a bomb will be thrown on those pigs. They've sucked our blood long enough."

"The planning was perfect. If a stray bullet hadn't hit your leg, they'd never have caught you."

"True. What did you do, you and Mustapha?"

"We stayed up till morning, feeling miserable."

He laughed briefly. "Weren't you afraid that I'd confess?"

"Mustapha urged me to flee with him; then we thought of

hiding. We went through a few miserable days. But you proved to be superhuman. We were and remain nothing."

As a man gets used to hell, he gets used to the sacrifice of others. However disgusting the rat is, the sight of him in his cage is pitiable.

Othman alluded to the assistance his parents had received from Omar before their death. Omar seemed not to want to listen, so he went on. "I don't want to lament the past, for I chose my fate, fully conscious of what I was doing. But now you must tell me what's been happening in the world."

Omar said enigmatically, looking for an escape, "Let the future be our main concern."

"The future? . . . Yes, I'll have to dust off my law degree."

"My office is at your disposal."

"Excellent. The authorities have no objection to my practicing."

"Then why not start right away?"

"Many thanks . . . but tell me what's been happening."

He doesn't want to budge. How strange, it's as though you'd never been associated with him, as though you'd never wanted this meeting at all. You share nothing but a dead history, and he arouses in you only feelings of guilt, fear, and self-contempt. He hasn't yet discovered that philosophical works have replaced the socialist tracts in your library. Here he sits obstructing you like fate while you try to flee from your people and from the world.

Tiring of the silence, Othman coaxed, "Tell me about our friends."

"Oh, they're all gone their own ways. I haven't kept up with any of them except Mustapha al-Minyawi."

"And what have you all done?"

How distasteful is this calling to account.

"Actually the years that followed your arrest were characterized by so much violence and terrorism that we had to resort to silence. Then each of us became involved in his work, we grew older, the Revolution broke out, and the old world collapsed."

Othman rested his broad chin on his hand, and his eyes gleamed coldly. Perhaps he was lamenting the lost years. What an unpleasant situation! How often the thought of it had disturbed his sleep like a nightmare. He said, "I often asked myself why, yes why, and it seemed to me that life was a revolting swindle. The feet that kicked in my head belonged to the very people for whose sake I went to prison. Were cowardice and folly, then, what life was all about? But this wasn't true of the ants and other creatures. I won't prolong the speech. In the end I regained my faith."

"How unfortunate."

"I rediscovered my faith hewing rocks under the sun. I affirmed to myself that my life had not been wasted, that millions of unknown victims since the time of our forebears, the apes, have raised man to a lofty position."

Omar bowed his head in respectful agreement, as Othman continued in an agitated voice. "It's stupid to get caught up in a sick past while the future rises before us, a million times stronger than our cowardice."

He looked for some means of escape from the onrush. "In any case, the corrupt world of the past has been destroyed by a genuine revolution, so one of your dreams has been realized."

How morose and sullen his face has grown. Here you are, swallowing defeat in an area which doesn't interest you at all. Doesn't he realize you no longer care about anything?

Othman said ruefully, "If you hadn't rushed into hiding, you wouldn't have lost the field."

"We had neither power nor any followers among the people to speak of. If, by some miracle, we'd succeeded, continents would have risen to destroy us."

"It's unfortunate that the ill only think of disease."

"Do you think it is reasonable for them to ignore it?"

"No, it's mad, not reasonable, but haven't you realized how much the world owes to madness?"

He said mildly, "In any case, the Revolution has occurred, and is going in the direction of genuine socialism." Othman scrutinized him closely, and Omar didn't like what he saw in his expression. "Though it didn't touch the heads of capitalists like me, it imposed a just tax." He concluded lamely. "Believe me, I'm not a slave of anything. Let them all go to hell."

Othman smiled. "Be frank with me, my dear friend. Are you a true believer as you once were?"

Put on the spot, Omar thought for a while. "I was until the Revolution broke out, then I felt reassured, began losing interest in politics, and turned in another direction."

"Another direction?"

He said hesitantly, "Mustapha is fond of describing it as an irrepressible nostalgia for my artistic past."

Othman asked impatiently, "And is there any contradiction between art and principle?"

Annoyed and perplexed, he answered, "It's not that simple."

Othman despaired. "I understand only that you're not what you were."

So Zeinab and Warda have remarked. "I admit you shouldn't concern yourself with me." Then he said more positively, "What's important now is to start a new life, in compensation for the past."

"I'm afraid I won't find anything that can really compensate for the past."

"My office is at your disposal, with all that you need to get started."

"I don't know how to thank you."

"It's far less than you deserve. I will always be indebted to you." Then in a voice quite free of constraint, he suggested, "No doubt you're longing to see Zeinab, the family, and Mustapha. Let's all have dinner at home tonight."

SIXTEEN

The dinner party was as rich in memories as it was in food and drink. Zeinab pressed his hand in welcome, her eyes brimming with tears, and Mustapha gave him a warm hug. It was the first time he'd seen Aliyyat. As he sat next to Buthayna at the table, he remarked with surprise that she was the picture of her mother as a girl.

"I can't possibly taste all of them!" he said as the appetizers were offered. Then he turned to Buthayna. "They told you I was an old friend, but that is only a partial truth. Actually, I'm an old friend who's just gotten out of prison."

She smiled, taking it as a joke.

"It's true. I'm an old friend and a veteran prisoner."

At this point, Zeinab intervened. "Then she should know that you're a political hero, not merely a prisoner."

Buthayna looked at him with astonishment.

"Hero. Criminal. The words are interchangeable."

Omar said to her, "Othman is an old friend, and now a colleague in the firm. I'll tell you his story another time. But you already know something about the political prisoners . . ."

"Did the King imprison you?" Buthayna asked.

As the houseboy was placing a slice of turkey and some peas on his plate, he said, "No, the whole society did."

"What had you done?"

When he didn't answer, Mustapha laughed. "He was a socialist prematurely." Then he added with a wink, "And he was fond of playing with bombs."

The green eyes widened, and Zeinab stepped in again, trying tactfully to change the subject. "Buthayna is a poet."

Othman looked at Omar and smiled. "Poetry is hereditary in this family."

Mustapha warned him, "Her poems are paeans of praise to the Divine Spirit!"

Restraining the urge to say something sarcastic, he commented politely, "I hope to have the good fortune to hear some of your poems."

Omar managed to hide his restlessness and maintain the appearance of calm. He took a stuffed pigeon, reflecting that if it had flown better, it wouldn't have been eaten, and followed with pleasure the conversation between Buthayna and Othman. Suddenly the girl asked, "How could you endure prison life?"

"I endured it because I had no choice, and I came to be known for my good conduct. It seems that we only misbehave in society." He laughed. "Actually, prisons are not without their advantages. Life among prisoners is classless, something we'd like to achieve in the world outside."

"I don't understand a thing!"

"You'll understand my words if I'm able to understand your poetry."

"Have you read Papa's poems?"

"Of course."

"Did you like them?"

Omar protested. "For God's sake, you'll never finish dinner if you don't stop talking."

But Othman continued, obviously enjoying her conversation. "Will you study literature in the university?"

"Science."

"Bravo, but why science when writing poetry is your main interest?"

Zeinab said proudly, "She excels in science."

Buthayna explained, "Papa's enthusiastic about studying science."

Othman looked at Omar quizzically, then said to Buthayna, "One day you'll realize science is the great hope."

"But I won't give up poetry."

"And why should you?"

"How many years did you spend in prison?"

"About twenty."

He laughed at her astonished expression. "And yet I knew a man who did not want to leave jail. Every time the date of release drew near, he'd commit another small crime, just to prolong his imprisonment."

"What a crazy way to behave."

"How often people behave in crazy ways."

"Don't you want him to eat?" Omar reproached her.

Othman and Buthayna continued their conversation after they'd all adjourned to the parlor for coffee. But around ten o'clock, at Mustapha's suggestion, the three men went out to the balcony, and the women moved to the living room.

Othman wanted to know what Mustapha had done with his life, so he gave him a frank, rather jaded account and concluded by asking, "What are your thoughts, now that you've heard what our situation is?"

Othman replied, a bit apathetic and sullen after Buthayna's

disappearance, "I'll have to get started as a lawyer, first of all."

"Yes, but I'm asking what's going on in your head."

"I'll have to study the conditions . . ."

"As you should, but our old position is no longer really valid."

"It is valid," he said defiantly.

"I mean that the state is now socialist. Isn't that enough?"

Omar looked in silence at the flowing river and at the reflections of lamplight on the surface. A crescent moon was visible on the horizon.

Othman said bitterly, "Just because you have changed doesn't mean truth has changed."

"We haven't changed so much as developed."

"Backward."

"The country has certainly gone forward."

"Maybe, but you've gone backward."

Omar was still looking at the moon as Mustapha said jokingly, "Aren't you satisfied with what you've already sacrificed of your life?"

"Truth is never satisfied."

"My dear friend, it's not your responsibility alone."

"Man shoulders the burden of humanity as a whole, or else he's nothing."

Mustapha laughed. "If I can't shoulder the burden of Mustapha, how could I take on humanity as a whole?"

"How pathetic . . . I can't believe how degenerate you've both become."

Mustapha couldn't take the conversation seriously, but, pointing to Omar, he said, "Let Omar be, for he's going through a bad time. A revulsion from work, success, and the family."

Othman looked inquiringly at Omar, but his head was still turned toward the Nile.

"As if he's searching for his soul," Mustapha observed.

Othman frowned. "Wasn't it he who lost it?" Then he sighed. "So it's all ended in philosophical meditations."

Mustapha went on, trying to restrain his mirth. "I've often felt that he wanted to revive his dormant impulse to write, and he continues to try. But he dreams sometimes of a strange ecstasy."

"Can you be more explicit?"

Omar turned toward them. "Drop the subject and just consider it an illness."

Othman looked at him sharply and murmured, "Perhaps it really is a disease, for you've lost your old vigor."

Mustapha said, "Or he's searching for the meaning of his existence."

"When we're aware of our responsibility toward the masses, the search for a personal meaning becomes quite insignificant."

Omar asked with irritation, "Do you think the question will die when the dictatorship of the proletariat is established?"

"But it hasn't been established yet." He looked from one of them to the other. "Scientists search for the secret of life and death through knowledge, not through illness."

"And if I'm not a scientist?"

"At least you shouldn't throw the dust of wailing and lamentation in the faces of the workers."

Mustapha said, "You're hurling some strong language at our friend at a time when he really is in pain."

"I'm sorry, and I'm afraid I'll have to remain sorry indefinitely."

Omar asked, "Won't the heart come to our rescue if we're not scientists?"

"The heart is a pump operating through the arteries and veins. To see it as a means of apprehending the truth is sheer fantasy. Honestly, I'm beginning to understand you. You're looking for ecstasy, or perhaps for something called absolute truth, but because you lack any effective method, you turn to the heart as the rock of salvation. But it is only a rock, and with it you'll recede to the depths of prehistory. Your life will have been wasted. Even my life, spent behind prison bars, has not been sacrificed for nothing. But your life will be. You'll never attain any truth worth speaking of except through reason, science, and work."

He hadn't witnessed the desert sunrise, or felt the ecstasy which gives assurance without proof. The world had not been cast, like a handful of dust, beneath his feet.

Mustapha said, "I believe in science and reason, but I have in my hands a *kasida** which Omar wrote just before renouncing poetry for good. In it, he declares his revolt against reason."

Controlling himself, Othman said, "I'd like to hear it."

Omar was about to protest, but Mustapha had already unfolded the paper, and begun to read:

> *"Because I neither played in the wind*
> *Nor lived on the equator*

*An ancient Arabic form of poetry.

Nothing charmed me but sleeplessness
And a tree which doesn't bend to the storm
And a building which doesn't shake."

A heavy silence reigned until Othman spoke. "I didn't understand any of it."

Omar said, "And I didn't say it was poetry, just hallucinations while I was in a morbid frame of mind."

Mustapha observed, "But modern art in general breathes this spirit of rebellion."

Othman said disdainfully, "It's the whimper of a dying order."

"Perhaps that's true," Mustapha said, "but speaking as a veteran artist, I see an artistic crisis as well, the crisis of an artist who is fed up with his subject matter and searching for a new form."

"Why should he be fed up with the subject matter?"

"Because whatever subject he hits upon is hackneyed."

"But the artist confers his own spirit on the subject which makes it new to a certain extent."

"This no longer suffices in our era of radical revolutions. Science has ascended the throne and the artist finds himself among the banished entourage. However much he wanted to penetrate the lofty realm, his ignorance and inability prevented him, and so he joined the Angry Young Men, turned to the anti-novel and to the theater of the absurd. While scientists were compelling admiration through their incomprehensible equations, the silly artists strove to impress by producing obscure, strange, and abnormal effects. If you can't attract the public's attention with your profound thoughts, try running naked through Opera Square."

Othman laughed loudly for the first time.

"Therefore I've chosen the simplest and most honest route, and become a clown."

Why get involved, Omar concluded, in discussing matters of no concern to him?

SEVENTEEN

The dawn was speechless. On the banks of the Nile, on the balcony, even in the desert, the dawn was speechless. And nothing but a broken memory bore witness to its ever having spoken. There's no point in continuing to look upward, burning the heart out, listening to its cries of yearning reverberate hopelessly in the heavens. The nagging rhymes, Margaret's golden hair, Warda's gray eyes, and the image of Zeinab leaving church. What are they but pale ghosts wandering in a hollow head? Mustapha laughs, tolling the death of hope, while Othman rages like a prophet of nihilism. I've spoken to the chairs, the walls, the stars, and the darkness; I've argued with the void, I've flirted with something which doesn't yet exist, until I finally found comfort in the prospect of my complete annihilation. Everything has been demeaned, the very laws that rule the universe have been discredited, predicting even the sunrise is impossible. After this how can I peruse the case files or discuss the household budget?

I said to the four walls of my room, "What a mistake it was to accept this truce and return home."

And I told the cat who was rubbing against my leg, "Your word is my command. I'll leave this refuge, so full of emotions which disturb and inhibit."

No diversions were left, other than dancing on the peak of the pyramid, plunging from a bridge into the depths of the Nile, or breakfasting nude at the Hilton. Rome was set aflame by desperate passions, not by Nero. They cause the earth to quake, the volcanoes to erupt.

Warda spoke on the telephone. "I wonder whether you've forgotten my voice."

He answered listlessly, "Hello, Warda."

"Won't you visit us even once a year?"

"No, but I'm at your service if you need anything."

"I'm speaking to you from the heart."

"The heart," he scoffed, "is a pump."

He sought relief from distress by speeding like a madman to the outskirts of Cairo, and further on to Fayum, Tanta, and Alexandria. Often he would leave Cairo in the morning and return the next day, having roamed around all night. He might go into a grocer's for a drink or doze off briefly at a café, or he might join a funeral procession, honoring some unknown deceased, and when he returned at dawn, overcome by fatigue, he would sleep right in the car or on the banks of the Nile.

He went back to the office one day and found Othman zealously working away.

"Where have you been these past days?" the man asked.

He looked at him disparagingly. "Innumerable places."

"You must be tired. I wonder what's going on in your head."

His distress had freed him of self-consciousness and fear, even in confronting Othman. "I'm thinking of exploding the atom, or murdering if that fails, or committing suicide at the very least."

Othman laughed. "But your office."

"You've been with me long enough to understand me."

"Tell me what you plan to do."

He said decisively, "It's time to do something I've never done before—that is, to do nothing."

"You must be joking."

"I've never been more serious."

Omar's stern expression caused Othman to change his tone. "Have you consulted your doctor?"

"I won't consult anyone on something of which he's ignorant."

An oppressive silence fell. "And you, are you confining your energies to the practice of law?" Omar finally asked.

"Yes, but I haven't stopped thinking."

"So, you'll become once more a menace to the country's security."

Othman smiled. "I can't claim that honor yet."

Really, this buzzing going on around him made it impossible to listen to the silence. He would have to leave, and his nerves were so on edge, he could no longer trust himself to keep silent about confidential matters. So he told Zeinab that he would give her power of attorney over his property, and leave his associates in charge of the office. He was determined, he said, to rid himself of distractions, to remove the burden of the world from his shoulders. She should consider it a disease, whether she understood it or not. In any case, he wanted to withdraw into himself. There was no woman involved, she must believe him. And it was not a mere whim; rather his illness had reached crisis proportions. If any cure existed, it lay in the path he'd chosen.

She implored him, her eyes reflecting the pain of the successive blows she'd received. "We've let you alone. If you can't stand your work, then leave it. If your artistic urges are so strong, then follow them. But don't desert us, for the sake of your children."

Her words affected him, but he said there was no use in trying to put off a decision as unavoidable as fate. "I've had long talks with Mustapha. It hurt me that you've confided in him what you've hidden from us, but I suppose in your present condition, you're not to be blamed. Forgive me for not understanding this search for the meaning of your existence. I don't see why it involves leaving your work and your family, disregarding your future. Why don't you consult your doctor again?"

"That's why I haven't been open with you."

"But illness isn't shameful."

"You think I'm insane."

She sobbed convulsively, but he remained resolute, "The solution I've chosen is best for us all."

"All right, then, leave until you've regained your health, but then return."

"It's best to reconcile ourselves to a permanent absence." He continued as she wept. "If I don't do that, I'll go mad or commit suicide."

She stood up, saying, "Buthayna's not a child. You must listen to her."

"Don't make the torment any worse," he shouted.

He could imagine what was being said about his "illness," but what difference did it make? Perhaps the diagnosis was even true. He talked to the animals and objects around him, and held discussions with extinct creatures. Sometimes when he was racing along in the car, the solid earth would explode into fragments, then disintegrate into a vast network of atoms, and, trembling uncontrollably, he'd have to stop. Sometimes as he was gazing at the Nile or at a tree it would come alive, the image would assume features which indicated feelings and awareness, and he'd imagine that it peered at him warily, that it questioned his existence in comparison with its own, so much more ancient and immutable. What did it all indicate? What did his desertion of work, family, and friends signify? Ah, he'd have to be on guard or else he'd find himself driven to the insane asylum.

Mustapha and Othman came to see him, at the urging of Zeinab, he realized. Mustapha's laughter failed to ease the tension. Omar himself barely murmured a greeting, but when the whiskey was brought out, he took a drink in their honor. They looked at him awkwardly, revealing the concern they'd striven to conceal. Zeinab then came out to greet the men, and commented as she was leaving, "We were such a happy family, he was the best of men, then suddenly everything fell apart."

Her words made it impossible to avoid the subject any longer. "Is what we've heard true?" Mustapha asked.

He didn't answer, but his determined expression was sufficient confirmation.

"So, you're leaving."

"Yes," he said sharply.

"Where?"

"Somewhere."

"But where?"

He remained silent. The place, stretching on to infinity, was still a prison. Mustapha was stupid to use words without meaning.

"So now it's our turn to be thrown on the garbage heap."

"Yesterday Buthayna cried, but that was the only answer she got."

"Is it the end of our relationship with you?" Mustapha asked fearfully.

"It's the end of my relationship with everything."

"What I've suffered is worse."

"And to what end?" Mustapha asked.

"To ram my head against the rock," he answered bitterly.

"I don't understand," said Othman.

Mustapha continued. "Whatever it is, stay among us."

Othman said, his eyes fixed on Omar, "Shouldn't you consult the doctor?"

"I'm not in need of anyone," he replied sharply.

"You're an intact organism which shouldn't be destroyed to no purpose."

"In reality, I'm nothing."

"Can't a man think while he's among other people?"

"I don't care about thinking."

"What will you do, then?"

He said with annoyance, "We don't understand each other at all."

"But I'm sure that you're driving yourself to ruin."

"Rather, it's you who are on the way to ruin."

"Well, if ruin is unavoidable, isn't it better to go down together?"

He brushed the remark aside. "I won't look back."

"In fact, you're running after nothing."

Is the ecstasy of the dawn nothing? Does truth then lie in nothingness? When will the torture end?

"Imagine if all the intelligent men in this world followed your example," Othman said.

"Let the intelligent men concern themselves with the world."

"But you're one of them."

He wiped his forehead, then thrust his fist toward the ground. "Trample my mind under your feet," he said disdainfully.

Othman asked sadly, "What's the use in arguing?"

"It's futile, for tomorrow you won't see me."

Mustapha sighed. "I don't believe a word of what's been said."

He answered, his eyes on the ground, "It's best for you to forget that I ever existed."

"It's too hard to bear," Mustapha said.

Othman's face hardened with suppressed grief, while Omar assumed a mask of indifference. As he gazed at them, their figures disintegrated into two groups of atoms, effacing their individuality, but the conflict he felt showed that his love for them, as for his family, was still rooted in his heart, causing him more anguish than he could bear. How his soul longed for the moment of victory, the moment of complete liberation!

EIGHTEEN

When your heart achieves its desire, you will have transcended the confines of time and space. But you still feel oppressed in this cottage, in the midst of a grassy lawn surrounded by a fence lined with cypress trees. And you await the day when the cypresses and all they enclose will disappear, the day when the plants will no longer whisper of the night's sorrows, the day when the scuttling of the cockroaches and the croaking of the frogs will fall silent, the day when memory will lose its tyranny and you'll merge into nothingness. Then the chants of India and Persia will no longer echo and the rosy beams of ecstasy will fall directly upon you. That precious, hard-won ecstasy of dawn will draw you with all the force of the unknown into heaven's dome, where your heart will awake while the bodily senses sleep.

Buthayna stood in front of him, like a graceful cypress, and turned her green eyes to the garden, to the canal running between the acacia trees, and to the fields stretching beyond. "For the sake of this?" she asked reproachfully.

Affected by her presence, you stroked the wavy locks of her hair and murmured, "For the sake of nothingness."

"Aren't you afraid of loneliness in this empty place?"

You whispered in her ear, "I was oppressed by loneliness in the midst of the crowds."

She retreated a step. "Yesterday, Othman said . . ."

He interrupted her gently. "My girl, haven't you realized yet that I'm deaf?"

She left the garden through the wooden gate in the ivy-covered fence and vanished from sight. I sighed wearily and opened my eyes to the dark. This dream could only mean that I've not yet escaped the call of life. However often I think of you during my waking hours, these weird fantasies mock my sleep.

Mustapha embraced you affectionately and then peered sadly into your eyes. You noticed that on his bald pate there now grew a heavy black shank of hair and couldn't help remarking, "Congratulations. How did you manage to grow it?"

He answered with unaccustomed seriousness. "I recited the 'All-Merciful Sura' at dawn."

You were astonished. "When did you find your way to God?"

"When you departed from the world for this place."

"Why did you come?"

"To tell you that Zeinab is working with the energy of ten men."

"God help her!"

He looked around at the house, the garden, and the fields. "What an ideal love nest or artist's retreat this place is!"

Nonplussed, you said, "So you're still the jester!"

He sighed. "For us children of the Stone Age, jesting is the only recourse, but I see you've become infatuated with despair."

I backed off, saying, "Haven't you realized that my senses are dead?"

He shrugged his shoulders and climbed up a cypress tree until he'd overtaken the current moon high above the horizon. His bald head glimmering in the moonlight, he shook a bell in his hand, and as it rang, insects of all sorts came to the tree and proceeded to dance in a circle around it.

I sighed wearily and opened my eyes to the dark. This dream could only mean that I've not yet escaped the call of life. However often I think of you during my waking hours, these weird fantasies mock my sleep.

Yesterday as I was roaming around the garden, reciting the poetry of Majnun, I suddenly heard a gruff voice coming from behind the northern wall where the canal runs.

"Hey, man, where's the door?"

Peering over, I saw Othman perched on a motorcycle. Little flags, the sort used by people of the village for decoration on feast days, embellished the handlebars and wheels.

"Don't come in," I said peremptorily.

"Haven't you witnessed the miracle?" he exclaimed. "I've crossed the surface of the canal by motorcycle."

"I don't believe in miracles."

He laughed loudly. "But we live in an age of miracles."

I retreated a step. "What do you want?"

He said augustly, "I've come as the family delegate."

"I have no family."

"Don't you know of the miracle? New branches of your family have appeared on all five continents. Wouldn't you like to return to that remarkable mixture of platinum and coal?"

I defied him. "Aren't you aware that our real family is nothingness?"

"I'm going to chase you with a pack of trained dogs," he said menacingly.

As the motorcycle roared and the dogs yelped, I sighed wearily and opened my eyes to the darkness. This dream could only mean that I've not yet escaped. However often I think of you during my waking hours, these weird fantasies mock . . ."

I stayed up all night in the garden, alone in the darkness with the stars shining overhead in the dome. I asked them when my desires would be fulfilled, and shouting so that the atoms of the cypress tree shook, reprimanded both everything and nothingness.

"I want to see," I said, gazing at one of the stars.

"Then look," it whispered.

I looked and found only emptiness. This is not the vision I've yearned to see.

"Look," it whispered.

The darkness lifted from the figure of a naked man. He was savage in appearance with shoulder-length hair and held a stone club in readiness to fight. Suddenly a wild beast sprang upon him. It was an unrecognizable species; though it resembled a crocodile, it stood on four legs and had the face of a bull. A bloody battle ensued between them, but in the end the beast was vanquished and the man staggered away. Blood splotched his face and chest and flowed from his arms, yet pain did not prevent him from smiling.

But this is not the image I've yearned to see, as you well know.

"Look," it whispered.

The darkness faded, revealing an open space in the forest

at the bottom of a mountain. Mountain men armed with stones rushed into the clearing and were opposed by men of the forest, equally fierce, equally ready for the kill. They fought ferociously. The flowing blood and frenzied screams so frightened the wild animals that they fled for refuge in the canals, in the treetops, and up the mountain. Eventually the forest men were routed, killed, or taken prisoner, and the mountain men made merry.

Nor is this the image I've yearned to see.

"Look," it whispered.

I saw nothing at first, but then a sudden surge of happiness filled my heart, a sudden sense of victory. I remembered the glowing sensation which preceded the other revelation, that dawn in the desert, and I was sure that ecstasy was approaching, and that the bridegroom's face would break forth as the music played. The darkness lifted from a scene which gradually became clearer and more distinct and my heart throbbed as it never had before. I saw a bouquet, not of roses, but of human faces, and I was stunned when I recognized them— the faces of Zeinab, Buthayna, Samir, Jamila, Othman, Mustapha, and Warda. Suddenly my fervor abated and I felt bitter disappointment in its place. This is not the vision I've yearned to see. You know that very well. Where is it, where is it? But the vision held fast and only grew sharper with time. Then the figures played tricks. Zeinab and Warda exchanged heads. Othman had Mustapha's bald pate, while Mustapha looked at me with Othman's eyes. All at once Samir slid to the ground, and putting on Othman's head in place of his own, started crawling toward me. Frightened, I tried to escape this hybrid of Samir and Othman, but the faster I ran, the faster he pursued me. I jumped over the garden fence, but like a cricket, he cleared it with a hop. I ran along-side the canal, but like a stubborn bull, he followed in my tracks. Out of breath, my muscles aching with fatigue, and my head in a spin, I collapsed to the ground, and as I lay face down on the damp grass, I heard the feet of the creature coming closer and closer.

The devil has played havoc with the dream. Ecstasy has become a curse, and paradise a stage for fools. I lay there submissively, no longer trying to resist, then raised my head slightly to look around. A willow recited a line of poetry, a cow approached and stated she was giving up the milk business in order to study chemistry, a spotted snake crept for-ward, darted out his poisonous fang, then proceeded to dance merrily. A fox stood upright, guarding the chickens, a choir of beetles sang an angelic hymn, and a scorpion confronted me, wearing a nurse's uniform.

I sighed wearily and opened my eyes to the darkness. This dream could only mean that ... However often I think of you during my waking hours ...

NINETEEN

I lay on the grass, gazing up at the trees which swayed in the darkness, and resolved to wait as long as necessary. Suddenly I heard steps approach and a voice whisper, "Good evening, Omar."

A ghost loomed up beside me. Another dream, and yet I fail to perceive anything.

"I'd almost lost hope of finding you. Why are you lying here? Aren't you afraid of the damp?"

He sat down on the grass and stretched his hand toward me. I ignored it.

"Haven't you recognized me yet? Have you forgotten my voice?"

I groaned. "When will the devil let me rest in peace?"

"What are you saying, Omar? For God's sake, talk to me, for I'm very upset."

"Who are you?"

"How strange! I'm Othman Khalil!"

"What do you want?"

"It's Othman, don't you understand? What I should have avoided has happened, and now I'm being chased."

I felt him with my hand. "But this is not Samir's body. What guise have you come in this time?"

"Samir? . . . You frighten me!"

"But you won't frighten me. I won't go tearing off like a madman."

He touched me, "Talk to me, for God's sake, as a friend. Don't make me despair of you!"

"What does that matter?"

"Listen, Omar, I'm in a bad situation. They're looking for me everywhere. If they catch me I'll die."

"So it's you who's running away this time."

"I'm going to hide at your place until it's safe to run."

I asked sadly, "How did the devil know I was here?"

"We've known your whereabouts all along—not a hard thing for a journalist like Mustapha to track down. He often comes around here, asking the peasants who bring your food to keep an eye on you. We didn't want to disturb you."

I groaned. "It's they who've blocked his face from me."

"During the past year and a half we haven't once disturbed you."

"I don't care even if Samir's head has been replaced by yours."

He sighed sorrowfully. "What's happened to you? No, I refuse to believe that you haven't recognized me yet."

"You can believe it or not."

"Pay attention to me, Omar, I have some startling news for you. I've married Buthayna."

"Let the devil go ahead and play his tricks."

He stuck his face in front of mine. "In spite of the difference in age, we got married, for we love one another, and now in her belly a new life throbs, my son, your grandson!"

"As you have been both my son and my enemy!"

"Hasn't this incredible news awakened you?"

"Like the snake who darts out his fang and dances."

"What a pity!"

"That's what I always say, but no one replies."

He patted my shoulder. "Come back down to earth. I've escaped just in time. They're combing the place for me now; they've searched your office and may try to implicate you. Go back, clear yourself, and look after your family. They're in great need of you. Buthayna's expecting a child and will never see me again ..."

"And I have never seen him."

"Don't you want to understand?"

"I die a score of deaths every day in order to understand, but still I've not understood."

"Can't you understand that I'm married to your daughter and that I must hide or else die?"

"Run until you drop from fatigue, then you'll hear the beetles sing."

"How awful!"

"Yes, it's awful."

He shook me and said angrily, "Wake up. This is not the time for hallucinations. I must make you understand before I leave."

"Go. Don't sully the purity of my dreams."

"How wretched! What have you done to yourself?"

"The devil is giving up on me."

"You must wake up. Your family is in danger. If suspicion falls on you, they'll be exposed to all sorts of abuse. I don't fear for myself, I'm resigned to my own downfall, but you must get back to your family."

"Go back to hell where you belong."

Exasperated, he shook me once more. "I must run and you must go back."

"Stay, if you'd care to witness my victory."

He shook his head sadly. "What a fool you are. You've

wasted all your ability searching for something that doesn't exist."

"When will you realize that you don't exist?"

The man stood up. "I now attest that I've despaired of you, though the word 'despair' has been eliminated from my dictionary."

"There, the devil has given up . . ."

The specter retreated into the darkness, saying sadly, "Farewell, old comrade-in-arms."

The night was still once more, but suddenly the moon returned. "They've come. God knows how they found me so soon."

He ran through the garden toward the western wall, but soon fell back, shouting frantically, "I'm surrounded."

He ran to the cottage while I gazed up at the stars. But my peace was disturbed by a voice which shouted, "Give yourself up, Othman Khalil. Give up. You're surrounded on all sides."

There was no answer. I turned my eyes in the direction of the voice, but saw nothing in the darkness. "The devil persists in playing tricks, but I'm not surrounded. On the contrary, I'm free."

Voices came from all around the fence and gradually drew closer. One of them barked out, "Resistance is useless, meaningless."

The man in hiding didn't answer.

"There's meaning in everything," I murmured.

Suddenly the beam of a searchlight flooded the house with light. A noose was tightening around the place. "Give up, Othman," the voice shouted. "Come on out with your hands up."

"When will these infernal voices leave me alone?" I sighed.

But the dreadful voice persisted. "Don't you see that resistance is futile?"

"Nothing in this world is futile," I whispered.

The running footsteps and yelling voices went around to the back of the house. A specter lunged out onto the front porch, then screamed.

"It's over, he's been caught ... it's all over."

I whispered, "Nothing has an end."

Other specters now ran from the garden toward the house. One of them tripped over my leg and shouted as he fell, "Watch out! There are others."

A shot rang out and I moaned. It felt like a real pain rather than a dream confounded by the devil.

I sighed wearily and opened my eyes. This dream could only mean that I've not yet escaped. Why is it I think of you whenever I'm awake, yet these delusions mock my sleep? But wait. Where am I? Where are the stars, the grass, and the cypress trees? I'm riding in a car, lying on a stretcher, on the edge of which a man is perched. On the other side of the car, Othman sits in silence between two men. I must still be dreaming, but the pain in my shoulder causes me to moan.

"The bullet fractured his collarbone, but it's only a superficial wound. He's in no danger."

What is the meaning of this dream, where is it taking me? When will the pain in my shoulder ease up? When will the devil and his follies be put to flight? When will the world disappear from my dreams? I moaned in spite of myself.

"Be patient a little longer," a voice said.

I answered defiantly, "Disappear, so I can see the stars."

"You're going to be all right."

I said stubbornly, "I'll be all right when I succeed in vanquishing you."

"Calm down. The doctor will see you right away."

"I don't need anyone."

"Don't tire yourself by talking."

I said insistently, "The willow tree talks, snakes dance, and beetles sing."

He went on talking to himself in a low voice. He shut his eyes, but the pain persisted. When would he see the vision? Hadn't he deserted the world for its sake?

He had the feeling that his heart was beating in reality, not in a dream, and that he was returning to the world.

He found himself trying to remember a line of poetry. When had he read it? Who was the poet?

The line reverberated in his consciousness with a strange clarity: *"If you really wanted me, why did you desert me?"*

The leading Arabic novelist, Naguib Mahfouz was born in Cairo in 1911 and began writing when he was seventeen. A student of philosophy and an avid reader, he has been influenced by many Western writers, he says, including Flaubert, Zola, Camus, Dostoyevsky, and, above all, Proust. Until his retirement in 1972, Mahfouz worked in various government ministries—but he was always writing. Today he has more than thirty novels to his credit, among them his masterwork, the Cairo Trilogy. He lives in the Cairo suburb of Agouza with his wife and two daughters.